Panic in the Pits

A Thomas Ballard Mystery

D.G. Stern

Neptune Press
Visit our website:
www.neptunepress.org

This is a work of fiction. Names, characters, places and incidents either are the product of the author's imagination or are used fictitiously. Any resemblance to actual persons, living or dead, events or locales is entirely coincidental.

Printed in the U.S.A.

Publisher's Cataloging-In-Publication Data
(Prepared by The Donohue Group, Inc.)

Names: Stern, D. G., author.
Title: Panic in the pits / D.G. Stern.
Description: [Orlando, Florida] : Neptune Press, [2019] | Series: A Thomas Ballard mystery
Identifiers: ISBN 9781732455122
Subjects: LCSH: Gangsters--Death--Fiction. | Sheriffs--Florida--Fiction. | Automobile racing--Florida--Fiction. | Cocaine--Florida--Fiction. | Murder--Investigation--Fiction. | LCGFT: Detective and mystery fiction.
Classification: LCC PS3619.T477 P36 2019 | DDC 813/.6--dc23

What they are saying about the Thomas Ballard mysteries.

Stabbing Along the Straightaway

"D.G. captured every bit of the vintage world of racing world. It's a vivid picture with believable personalities and great cars, and one "who dun it" that will keep you guessing to the very end." —Jeanette Veitenheimer Lime Rock Park Historic Festival Executive Administrator

"You have a great understanding of the characters that have passion for the sport and the cars that they race. I enjoyed the book immensely. Great story." —Stephen Page Founder, Chairman and CEO Vintage Racing League

"Stern's sense of dialog and breezy style as well as his occasional spot on observations of the vintage racing scene make for a tough book to put down," —Vintage Sports Car

Chaos at the Concours

"Well-conceived and written. The Bentley Gang were in fine form. Many, many thanks for sharing your passion for all that is "collector cars" with me." —Stephen J. L. Page, Founder & CEO, Racing and Cars

"D. G. Stern masterfully shares with the reader the complicated inner workings of Ballard's thinking, revealing how he determined the motives for the murders and the evidence that led to a conclusion of what happened. It is obvious that Stern is a lover of vintage vehicles; he even has Ballard often residing in a vintage 1955 Airstream Flying Cloud travel trailer. Chaos at the Concours is fast-paced, exciting, and full of D. G. Stern's red

herrings. If you like murder mysteries, you will appreciate Stern's work." —AuthorsReading.com

"Stern's breezy and almost (but not quite) glib style is simply great fun and we recommend this one to any and all looking for a light novel with a motoring background to the story. It is assuredly a keeper." —Vintage Sports Car

Special Award

2018 First Place Books, Fiction
America Auto Racing Writers and Broadcasters
Association, Inc.

The winner ain't the one with the fastest car, it's the one who refuses to lose.

— *Dale Earnhardt*—

CHAPTER ONE

I can't believe it is only about five months, actually twenty-two weeks, nine days and seven hours, since I met Olivia Nederfield, but who is counting, and here I am wearing a tux and standing at the front of a church altar. Well, not exactly. I am standing toward the side of the altar, but Olivia is center stage-as the maid of honor for her best friend, Cynthia, who is marrying a really nice guy. At least she thinks so. I have only met him twice before. I alternate between joy and fear-joy for the about to be newlyweds and fear that getting married seems natural.

Having recently attended the fiftieth anniversary of some really dear people, Margarite and Hans Leiter, although the festivities were interrupted by the death of two people, I am beginning to get a warm and fuzzy feeling, like it's okay to feel warm and fuzzy. As a hardened reporter, and part time deputy sheriff, I try not to let my feelings get in the way. It's very difficult when you hang around someone as cool as Olivia Nederfield, who happens to be a full time Orange County (Florida) Sheriff's Detective.

My name is Thomas Ballard and I am a member of the fourth estate, a professional journalist, who writes about the thing I like best, besides Olivia, motor racing. I live in Central Florida when I am not on the road covering events, like the vintage car race at Citrus Grove Raceway where one of the drivers was stabbed to death. Or the Concours d'Elegance at the Indian Whisper Golf Course near Savannah, Georgia where two people met their demise at the same time, at the same place, in vastly different ways. And this was all in the last twenty-two weeks, nine days and a little more than seven hours. It is true that Olivia and I met professionally, and we have always respected that professionalism, even though we pretty much live together.

With no races to cover until tomorrow's Super Late Model race at the paved one-mile oval in Perrytown, about twenty five miles east of Orlando, I can relax and enjoy this special event. The journalist part is easy, just turn off my phone-no calls, texts or emails. Actually, as a journalist covering motorsports, I don't get many calls, texts or emails that require my immediate attention. The deputy sheriff part is also easy when I am with Olivia since it's her phone that is likely to ring. She's my boss. Her boss is Josh McCarthy, the Sheriff of Orange County, which includes Orlando, the Gateway to the attractions-Disney, Universal, Lego Land and a zillion smaller places for people to laugh and spend money. Josh is also my oldest friend. The chain of command does get a bit muddled sometimes, but we have found that we all work together very well-more or less.

I should probably concentrate on the service in case I ever need to remember how it's done. The first thing that strikes me is the smell of the flowers. In Florida we are, or at least were before the building booms, surrounded by the sweet scent of orange blossoms. You could land at Orlando International Airport and know you were home. The expression: *stop and smell the roses* or magnolias or honeysuckle has special meaning to those of us from the South who are blessed with fresh scents all year. It is hard to imagine winter in Maine having much smell-even the pine trees are frozen.

The wedding is over and I escort Olivia up the aisle, which is far different than escorting her down the aisle. The reception is being held at a vineyard about ten miles away. It is a very special place-not only do they make wine exclusively from blueberries, but they have goats and other livestock roaming around freely. Apparently the goats are fed some of the pulp from the blueberry fermenting process and are basically half in the bag all the time. They never wander off the farm. Must save a fortune on fencing.

Rather than opt for a ride in a limo, Olivia and I ensconce ourselves in her perfectly restored vintage Volkswagen beetle with the mandatory convertible top and leisurely cruise off to the wedding reception. I wonder if it can be a Bacchanalia if the wine is not made from grapes. No big deal. An afternoon and evening with Olivia is just fine with me.

"Thomas, would you dig my cell out of my pocketbook? I think it's vibrating."

I knew it was too good to be true. I start to excavate: wallet, badge, lipstick, compact, .38 police special with two inch barrel-blued not chromed, another lipstick and at last a cell phone, which has stopped vibrating. The screen displays the following message: *"You or Thomas call ASAP-Josh"*.

"It's the boss. He wants either of us to call." I don't know if I told him where we were going today. Maybe Olivia had to file her itinerary.

"I'm driving; you get to talk to Sheriff McCarthy."

"Gee thanks." I push the speed dial button. "At your service." I move the phone away from my ear so that I don't go deaf from Josh's less than modulated voice, and so Olivia can hear.

"Are you still dressed like a penguin?" He asks.

"Do you mean am I formally attired and am I riding with Detective Nederfield to a wedding reception?"

"Yeh."

"Both." I can be as terse as the next guy.

"Can you meet me at six?"

I look at Olivia, who shrugs.

"Where?"

"Headquarters."

"Do we need to change?"

"No, you two will fit right in."

"Do you want to give me some more information since we will be leaving the wedding reception of Olivia's best friend a tad early?"

"I'm doing you a big favor," the Sheriff continues.

"How so great wise one?"

"Ever think what would happen if Olivia caught the bridal bouquet?"

"Seven years bad luck?" I reply.

"No dummy, a whole life time."

Josh has been happily married forever, so he has no credibility regarding marital misery.

"Josh, we are pulling into the driveway at the reception, so give me a twenty second overview."

Olivia pulls into the first open parking space and ever so gently removes the phone from my hand and says in her big girl voice, "This better be good, Boss."

"Detective Nederfield, it's nice to hear your voice, too."

Although Olivia has only been with the Sheriff's office for a relatively short time, she has been promoted over a couple of other deputies to detective, but surprisingly and pleasantly everyone thinks she deserves it.

"Remember Cosmo Costello?" Josh asks. "I may be able to close a portion of your case load. His body was just recovered from the land fill. I need someone who knows the deceased to identify the body. I think the times you've spent together in the interrogation room should suffice."

I reclaim the phone from Olivia. "If he's dead, why can't this wait until tomorrow?"

"Because a rather large shipment of cocaine, which we believe was destined for Central Florida, has disappeared from our radar. The Coast Guard shadowed the shipment from Barranquilla, Columbia to Port Miami. DEA picked up the surveillance almost three weeks ago and followed the couriers to Homestead-Miami Speedway and then poof. We believe this may have contributed to the demise of the stiff I presume to be Cosmo. If the deceased is Costello, I can get search warrants and shake up some good ol' boys."

"Why not now?" Which I think is a reasonable question.

"Three reasons: the judge is playing golf and won't be available until 6; the coroner isn't done doing what coroner's do; and thirdly, I thought you and Olivia should have a relaxing afternoon. See you at six." Josh 'hangs up'.

CHAPTER TWO

I have only attended four weddings that I can remember, although my mother assures me I was adorable at her sister's wedding wearing gray flannel shorts and a starched and itchy white shirt with a little black bow tie. I rate the current event a 98. I am not sure what a 100 would be like, but as a writer I always tend to give myself some wiggle room in case I miss something. The ambiance is terrific, except for one very persistent goat who keeps pushing against my leg to announce that he or she is seeking attention-and food. Goats are really very funny looking. Their pupils are rectangular rather than round. It gives them the appearance of always laughing. Maybe the partially fermented blueberries add to that sense of mirth.

The bewitching hour, which in this case is a little after five o'clock in the afternoon, comes entirely too soon. But the Sheriff didn't seem to really care. I'm going to insist he give Olivia some time off, especially if the decedent is Cosmo. Maybe we can go to the Keys for a couple of days. Jimmy Buffett beware-I make a pretty wicked margarita.

Not withstanding that Detective Nederfield has her own marked parking space under the headquarters of the Orange

County Sheriff's Department, we raise and secure the top, roll up the windows, lock the doors and set the alarm. So much for anyplace being really safe.

"Are we really supposed to meet Josh wearing these clothes?" I ask.

"Don't you think I look nice?"

"Touché! But I, together with every other male . . . and a lot of females, have been showering you with compliments all day."

"A woman can never have enough praise heaped upon her."

"Is that like a woman can never be too thin or too rich?"

"Something like that."

Thank you Otis Elevator for arriving before I throw up. Only kidding. Olivia always looks fabulous-even in her green uniform, which fortunately she doesn't have to wear a lot being that she's a detective. I don't even have a uniform, but I do have a badge which says *SPECIAL DEPUTY,* whatever that means. Headquarters is a relatively new building which was actually designed by an architect. It is light and bright, uses a lot of glass (bullet proof no doubt) and stainless steel, and has signage that one can read (in multiple languages).

The Boss is standing, actually pacing, as we exit the elevator-drinking a Dr. Pepper. No surprise.

"Right on time," he says with no warmth.

I bet he had his weekend plans disrupted, as well. With two pre-teen sons who participate in every activity known to man, at a minimum Josh is missing a baseball game, soccer practice and maybe even a picnic. No wonder he is a bit grumpy. We are only missing blueberry wine, wedding cake, dancing in the moon light with slightly inebriated goats.

"You lead, we'll follow." I try to sound cheery.

Several young deputies approach Josh.

"Sir, I want to confirm that a room has been set up for the wedding reception." They start to laugh hysterically until six foot two inch Olivia Nederfield grabs one of the guffawing cops by the ear, kind of like my mother did.

"Sheriff, I think we need some company with us in the morgue. Maybe he can assist the M.E. on the midnight shift."

Now it is our turn to chuckle.

"Good idea Detective Nederfield," Sheriff McCarthy exclaims in his *I'm in charge* voice.

All three deputies are looking like their uniforms-a little green. Hanging out with dead bodies is not something you learn at the academy, nor do you ever get used to. We muddle on.

Medical examiners always have offices in the catacombs of police stations. I asked why on one of my too often visits. I was told, in all seriousness, *that it was closer to the loading ramp where the meat wagon drops off the bodies.* Actually it makes sense. The most distinguishing feature of the morgue is the smell. Antiseptic. Even with the infusion of lavender or citrus, the smell is unmistakable. Apparently, none of the young deputies has ever paid a visit to the *meat locker,* as it is often called and none looks the better for the visit.

I only had the privilege of meeting Cosmo Costello once. It was in connection with an article I was researching about gambling and professional car racing. He wasn't real helpful, but he also didn't have me killed. It didn't take Olivia long to ID the body on the steel gurney. No question that it was Cosmo.

Josh nods and we follow him out. The deputies try to follow. Sheriff McCarthy holds up his hand like a traffic cop. "I think the M.E. might have a few things you guys can do."

Speaking to the be speckled man in the white lab coat, Josh continues, "Stanley, these three men are anxious to provide you with any additional help you may need in performing an autopsy or two." If possible, the complexion of the three becomes even more green than before. I am not saying I don't feel a bit queasy, but watching dead bodies being opened, organs removed and weighed and listening to the patter of the coroner dictating his notes, is most definitely a downer.

Back on the ground floor, Josh says, "Give me a couple of minutes to get the wheels of justice moving. Hopefully I can get the judge to sign off, serve the search warrant, and find all sorts of great evidence before . . ." He looks at his watch. "Before Cheryl has dinner on the table. Oh, she insisted I invite you over. She been taking a course in Far Eastern cooking and tonight is Thai. Why don't you change into something less elegant and come by in about an hour."

When the Sheriff of Orange County invites you over for dinner, regardless of whether you have attended a wedding or a tennis match, it is a command performance. Having had dozens of dinners prepared by Josh's wife, the fare will undoubtedly be superb. I wonder if having just left the coroner's office is making me hungry. Food for thought. I am glad I talk to myself a lot.

"Can we bring anything?" Olivia thoughtfully asks.

"Just your appetite." Sheriff McCarthy is done with small talk, He starts to dial.

Olivia and I take this as our cue to leave.

We elect to head over to her house, which is closer than mine, although there is adequate clothing into which to change at both residences.

CHAPTER THREE

Dinner is as promised-fantastic. Cheryl has mastered the intricacy of balancing texture, smell, appearance and taste which is the foundation of great Thai food. The McCarthy boys are having a sleep-over at a neighbor's house, so dinner is peaceful and very collegial and focuses on everything except law enforcement, which must be a relief to our hostess. I know Olivia and I need time to chill out.

Since Olivia has decided to do domestic things tomorrow, I will be viewing the race at Perrytown solo. Sometimes doing one's own *thing* is a good idea. Sunday racing at small tracks is usually a family event. Often several generations come out to cheer on a friend or family member. It is definitely beer and hot dogs and good old boy racing. There is a lot of bumping of fenders, but few real accidents. I'm psyched.

The phone wakes me from a perfectly pleasant dream. What time is it? I grab the clock on my side of the bed and try to open my eyes. 7:15? Who calls at 7:15 on a Sunday morning?

"Hello." I suspect I sound a bit grumpy, because I am.

I move the phone away from my ear when I hear Sheriff McCarthy's melodious voice.

"Are you up?"

"I am now."

"They served the search warrant last night and got a lot of nothing. A few guns, some cash but no coke. Found some fresh blood stains on the front patio which are being examined as we speak."

"Tell me why this is important at this hour in the morning?" I think I am asking a fair question.

"Do you know who Don Montgomery is?" Josh is heading somewhere, but I am still too groggy to figure out where.

"He drives in the baby series. He may be in the majors by the end of the season." NASCAR, like major league baseball has both a major league and minor leagues. The baby series is like comparable to Triple A baseball-one step away from *the show.* But it is often a big step. "Why?"

"My guys found a picture of him with Cosmo, inscribed *to my patron and guardian.*"

"Any other connection?" I'm still trying to wake up so this conversation is not making a lot of sense.

"We think Cosmo may have been paying Montgomery," Josh continues.

"For what?"

"Good question. Did your racing and gambling investigation turn up anything?"

"Thomas, is that who I think it is?" Olivia asks.

"Josh, the long and the short is that Montgomery is still small potatoes and even if he threw a race, there's no real money in the baby series. Now my friend, if you don't mind, I need to get up, shower and shave and head off to Perrytown for the Super Late Model feature. Maybe even a beer or two. I have decided to do a fashion feature focusing on tee-shirts worn at race tracks."

"Have you looked outside?" Sheriff McCarthy is talking in circles. "It's pouring. A front from the tropics will be soaking Central Florida all day."

I reluctantly climb out of bed and open the plantation blinds that Olivia and I installed last month. They really keep out unwanted light and noise. It is raining cats and dogs.

"Thank you for the weather report. I think that I am going to go back to bed and try to get Detective Nederfield to forgive you for rudely waking us up."

"Want to know what else we found?"

Olivia asks for the phone by snapping her fingers. "Boss, if there is something you want to say, please do so. Otherwise I am going to enjoy a leisurely, rainy Sunday morning."

"How about you guys meeting me at 10 for brunch at Betty's? My treat."

Olivia looks at me and since I have nothing to add, I shrug. "Make it 10:30. I'm going to read the paper."

"Done." Josh ends the call.

"Detective Nederfield requests the pleasure of Deputy Ballard to join her for another hour of sleep." She pats the bed. I accept, crawl under the covers and immediately fall asleep.

I am again awakened from a great dream, but this time it is to the smell of freshly brewed coffee. Olivia is puttering in the kitchen, wearing a British Racing Green terrycloth bathrobe monogrammed with a stylized yellow B, a gift from our dear friends, the Bentley Seven. Obviously Olivia has been up for a bit. Her hair is wrapped in a towel, the Sunday papers (we get several) are opened and I am greeted with a steaming mug of java.

"Good morning sunshine," she says, giving me a kiss on the cheek. But a meaningful kiss.

"I crashed," I say.

"Poor selection of words for an auto racing journalist."

"Probably so, but better than saying *I'd die for the cup of coffee* you are holding," I quip.

"Let's call a truce. We are butchering the King's English."

"Reminds me of Cosmo."

Olivia hands me the coffee and gives me another kiss. This time on the lips. Yes!

"I wonder what is bugging the Sheriff so much that he feels it necessary to invite us to Betty's." Olivia asks.

"Guess we'll find out soon enough. Can I have the sports section?"

We settle into pleasant quiet time, absorbing the ramblings of my print colleagues before dressing for brunch with the ogre.

CHAPTER FOUR

Betty's is just east of Orlando, but is in Brevard County, which is why Josh likes to go there. It's out of his jurisdiction. Betty's is a combination of a fish camp, roadside diner, honkey tonk bar with music every night and a 5–star restaurant. Located on the St. John's River, it is home base for a fleet (actually eight) air boats, which take out tourists into the river in hopes of spotting a 'gator. There are signs warning people to watch children and small dogs on the pier and never put your hand or foot into the water.

The vehicle of choice at Betty's is Harley Davidson, but sometimes a group of 60s and 70s muscle cars fill the parking lot. I once saw a Maybach with Palm Beach County license plates in the lot. The food is that good, especially brunch. Olivia graciously assents to me driving the VW despite the occasional showers. I ease it into a parking space under a giant live oak tree. In Florida, shade is the most important thing to consider when selecting where to park, although today's weather is rather gray and depressing.

We alight and enter into the Twilight Zone. Betty's was built in the 30s, rebuilt in the 40s, 50s and 60s and every decade thereafter as the ravages of hurricanes, floods and at least one tornado have attacked her weathered planks. The décor is period, but it is uncertain which period. The music is somewhat muted as a concession to Sunday, but the cacophony of sounds from patrons who have already consumed a six pack, is deafening and it's only 10:30. No one gets too loud or too drunk at Betty's and no one misbehaves. One strike and you are banned for life, which for this crowd is a very severe sentence.

When the sun is shining, as it frequently does in the Sunshine State, a lot of the crowd assembles on the wrap-around porch/deck. Alligators don't mind the music, I guess. Food is never thrown into the river. It promotes bad behavior from these prehistoric creatures.

Our hostess looks as if she comes from central casting-hair piled high on her head, bright red lipstick and chewing gum-but she is friendly. We are seated in the far corner of the main dining room in a booth for six, which is good when you are eating with Sheriff McCarthy, who we see enter, look around, point, nod and spritely move through the crowd to our table. He may be big, huge actually, but he is very agile.

"You look bright eyed and bushy-tailed," Josh says in an all too friendly voice.

"No thanks to you waking me up before sunrise," I reply.

"Now that we have all had our day interrupted by a dead man, what have you got Boss?" Detective Nederfield gets right to the point.

"The search warrant gave us some wiggle room so our guys were able to go through Costello's house, non attached garage and a storage garage he maintained at U-Store on Iris Avenue in Lake Judith. Other than a small bag of weed and a few pills which we believe were for Cosmo's personal consumption, the raid yielded very little. We found some guns, mostly Saturday night specials with no serial numbers and about $30,000 cash in small bills. No stash of cocaine."

"Nothing surprising and certainly not enough to get him killed," I suggest.

"You are withholding evidence Sheriff McCarthy," Olivia adds.

"Very astute Detective Nederfield."

As I am about to say something I probably shouldn't, our waitress appears and says, "Can I get you started with something to drink?" She looks like a clone of the receptionist except for a pencil pushed into her slightly blue tinted hair.

"I would like a Bloody Mary." Olivia does not hesitate in answering.

"Spicy or mild?"

"Spicy, please."

Josh and I look at one another and simultaneously say, "Me, too."

Our server leaves us each a menu, actually a single piece of paper, with today's selections. For me, it's a slam dunk, eggs Benedict and grits. Remember this is Florida and grits, like college football, are close to a religion.

"Out with it Sheriff." Olivia returns to the matter at hand.

"We are having our experts check Cosmo's computer. His cell was not recovered with the rest of his person, so it was either taken by his killer or killers or it is still somewhere in the dump. A GPS sweep of the area is being conducted as we speak. Maybe we will be lucky."

"Josh, all this you could have said over the phone," I observe.

"Other than the picture of Costello with Don Montgomery, we found a calendar which you might find interesting Thomas." Sheriff McCarthy hands me a standard monthly calendar exactly like the kind you get from the ASPCA, VFW or AAA except this one is a bit more graphic. I don't think Josh wants me to focus in on the scantily clothed girls. I know Olivia doesn't.

"Interesting. Very interesting."

"Out with it." Detective Nederfield is not always the most patient person around.

"The only scheduled appointments Cosmo has entered are car races in which it appears the beneficiary of his largesse, Don Montgomery, is racing." I respond. "He only lists the city or town in which the track is located, not the name of the track."

"That's what threw us off," Josh says.

"Do you think Costello was that much of a fan?" Olivia asks.

"Maybe he just liked the kid and was trying to provide some financial assistance." I think Josh is referring to the inscription on the photograph found at the decedent's house.

"Sheriff, was Cosmo's place tossed when your guys searched it?" Olivia is going somewhere, although I am not sure where.

"No, everything was neat and tidy, at least for a thug like Cosmo. Also all the food in the refrigerator was more or less fresh. No signs that Costello had been gone long or was planning a vacation."

"Any signs of a struggle?" Olivia continues.

"No, which is why we are assuming he may have met his demise on his own door step and was then moved. Two bullets at close range with a large caliber gun, probably with a silencer since no one reported shots." Josh is somewhat subdued.

"His car?" I decide to get into the conversation.

"In his garage. Half tank of gas, recently serviced, a .38 under the driver's seat and a pump action 12 gauge in the trunk."

"Do you think it is a fair assumption that someone he knew rang the door bell and killed him then and there?" Olivia is paging through the calendar and looks up for the Sheriff's answer, but as luck would have it, our drinks arrive.

"Are you ready to order?" The waitperson asks, between chomps on her gum.

"Please give us a couple of minutes." Josh tries to sound so nice, only somewhat successfully.

"Cheers," I say raising my glass. The others follow. Wow, it is spicy.

CHAPTER FIVE

Simultaneously, we look at the offerings on our menu. Nothing is changing my mind: eggs Benedict and grits. Our server keenly observes that we have each turned our menus up-side down, indicating that we have decided. She returns and asks, "I can take your orders."

Olivia selects a two egg omelet with spinach and tomato, while the Sheriff selects three eggs, easy over, bacon, English muffin and grits. One needs to keep the law enforcement engine filled with fuel. During the hiatus before our food arrives, I commit what I consider a very rude act-I look at my phone. I hadn't received any calls or texts. I simply wanted to check the finishing position of Don Montgomery at the events listed on the calendar. Nothing that I recall, so Google I must. Both Olivia and Josh are indulging me.

"Just as I thought. Montgomery's performance has been reasonably good this year. One win, three top five, eight top ten. He usually finished toward the front of the pack. Only one DNF. He didn't trash his equipment. Good to take note of a young driver like that."

"So Cosmo must not have been disappointed," Olivia adds.

"Josh, what about the comment you made that you thought the up and coming racer was receiving money from the decedent?" I ask.

"Each Monday following a race, Costello entered a figure on the calendar. We are trying to get an order to look at Montgomery's financial records."

I stare at the calendar more carefully and notice that a number followed by the letter "K" is written in very small print on the bottom right hand corner. The numbers range from 3 to 10-none higher.

Our server arrives with our meal, which smells heavenly. She quickly puts our plates in front of each of us and asks, "Anyone want something else to drink?"

I am embarrassed when I look at my Bloody Mary glass-empty. Olivia and Josh's drinks are also gone.

"Coffee black, please." Sheriff McCarthy sends us each a clear message-working breakfast.

"Same for me," Olivia follows.

"Unsweetened iced tea," I announce. Our server nods and leaves. "Before our breakfast gets cold, let's eat. I want to compare the figures on the calendar with Montgomery's finishing position in each race, although I have the gut feeling there is no connection."

During the next fifteen minutes we don't speak-we munch. There is something obvious that I am missing.

"Thomas, you look like you are deeply lost in your thoughts," Josh observes.

"Remember how you like to create a grid from the facts and then connect as many pieces as possible."

"You have been paying attention, haven't you?" The Sheriff can be sarcastic.

"You gave us no choice as I recall. Bread and water for two weeks." Olivia springs to my defense.

"It worked, didn't it? What's bugging you Thomas?"

"I just don't connect Cosmo Costello with Don Montgomery in any meaningful way," I answer.

"Boss, how soon can you get Montgomery's bank records?" Olivia asks.

"Not until tomorrow. I am having the search warrant prepared for the judge to sign in the morning. Then off to the bank or banks. Our IT guys are getting a list of any banking institutions Montgomery uses."

"What about Cosmo's banks?" I ask.

"I will have that checked out, but I sense he dealt primarily in cash," Sheriff McCarthy replies.

"Let us assume that Cosmo made payments to Montgomery in cash each week, in varying amounts, but none exceeding ten thousand dollars. How confident are you that Montgomery would put the money into a bank account?" Olivia is also trying to connect the dots.

"If Montgomery's prize money has been typically paltry this season, he still needs to live on something. The younger generation is keen on using their phones to pay for everything through the bank's app. In the end, there has to be money in the bank." I think my explanation makes sense, but why speculate when a lot more information will be available in the morning. Maybe I will order another Bloody Mary.

"Thomas, you raise an interesting point. There are two things that I think need our immediate attention: attend the race at the next venue at which Montgomery will be competing and order another Bloody Mary." The Orange County Sheriff is a pragmatic person.

"I agree with the latter and want to know where the former is taking place," Olivia opines.

"I also agree with the latter and according to the calendar Montgomery's next race will be taking place next weekend on the roval at Daytona."

"What is a roval?" Clearly, Josh has not been keeping up with automobile racing.

"A roval, my dear Sheriff, is the latest and maybe greatest thing that has happened to stock car racing in years. The track on which the cars participate is both a road racing course and the traditional oval track. The cars transition between the infield road circuit and the banked oval. It is exciting, different and very challenging."

"Whatever. You two will be in attendance. I'll talk to the Volusia County Sheriff's office and get you credentialed. Detective Nederfield, inasmuch as I have pretty much fouled up your weekend and next weekend as well, I will authorize you an additional week's vacation, at a time to be determined." The Sheriff seems pleased with himself.

"Wait a minute, I have a couple of questions," I begin. "Do I get an extra week of vacation, as well?

"Thomas, you are always on vacation, but I will give you the same week off I give to Detective Nederfield."

"With pay?"

"You will be paid exactly what we always pay you," the ogre replies.

"But you never pay me anything." I know I sound like I am whining.

"Exactly. But you have a nice shiny badge, right?"

The server once again arrives before I say something.

"Anything else?" She asks.

"Three more of your delicious Bloody Mary's . . . please." Sheriff McCarthy is simply too full of himself.

The Bloody Mary goes down very smoothly-almost too smoothly. I am troubled by my lack of background material relating to the dearly departed Cosmo Costello. I know that Olivia has been the lead detective on the department's team looking into his activities, but I need more data before connecting the dots. "Did either of you have any idea Costello was going to become a corpse?"

"Since I assume you mean, *why now?,* I don't have any clue."

"That's not much help, your sheriffness," I reply.

"Actually, I'd say the likelihood of Cosmo ending up in the morgue this weekend was very low. He was a made wise guy, with strong connections to Providence and Boston."

"Please explain so that a simple sports writer can follow," I ask.

"Most of the major Mafia crime families in the East get their orders from Providence, not New York or Boston. Hard to explain, but accept the fact that nothing happens without the OK from the Ocean State. Costello has always been a loyal foot soldier and as a reward for his loyalty, the bosses gave him Central Florida." Deputy Nederfield is speaking in hushed tones as if the room is bugged, which it may be.

"So Cosmo controlled all the mob's business activities here?" I am about to ask what those activities include when Olivia continues. She probably reads my mind. What do they say; *my mind is an open book.*

"Mostly drugs; opioids, cannabis and cocaine. Very little protection rackets or prostitution and gambling is pretty much controlled by the Seminoles. Costello wasn't a really big time operator like in South Florida, but was still the go to guy locally. But he was protected, so I don't think he was hit by anyone associated with the traditional mob."

"Are there other groups who might want less competition?" The dot connecting process continues.

"Sadly, the answer is yes. We have been following Cosmo for almost two years. Basically, the drug scene has been quiet. No gang related activity. Costello kept everything peaceful. Better for business. Unfortunately, the use of opioids has skyrocketed. The department has beefed up surveillance on known dealers in response to the increased demand which has given rise to increased violence," Sheriff McCarthy says. "Everyone wants a piece of the pie."

"Costello, for all his outward appearances of being a thug who controls a lot of muscle, was opposed to turf wars. There was always enough for everyone. He was very careful in his business operation and we never had quite enough for a solid collar. Also, as juxtaposed to many of Central Florida's newcomers, Cosmo looked for the inclusive path, not the polarizing path. He was respected by a lot of the underworld as an arbitrator of disputes. I don't want to make him appear as a hero, just a very savvy guy who didn't want attention drawn to himself or his activities." I think Olivia's description leaves me with more questions than answers.

"Let me throw this out. Cosmo was killed rather coldly, yet his house wasn't trashed, there were no signs of a struggle and he was likely unarmed. I think he knew and trusted whoever came to his house. Maybe he was trying to resolve a dispute and it didn't go well." I am groping for straws.

"Thomas, that is our conclusion as well. I think we will know a lot more about Cosmos's death when we examine his computer and cell phone. However the connection with a young race car driver remains a mystery. Hopefully, we will have additional information on all fronts tomorrow mid morning. I am less concerned about who killed Costello than why. I am petrified that Orange County could become a battlefield over control of the drug trade. Between protecting schools and everyday stuff like domestic violence, robbery, muggings, our department is stretched thin."

"Boss, do you really think that's possible?" Olivia's voices cracks just a bit.

"Yup. That's why we have got to fill in as many blanks as possible as soon as possible . . . but not today, since we don't want to drive ourselves crazy with supposition when we will have a lot more information tomorrow. Go home and read the paper or listen to music or whatever. See you at ten in my office." The Sheriff raises his hand to get the server's attention.

CHAPTER SIX

The thought of a potential drug war is not easy to put into the recesses of one's mind, even if that mind spends most of its time thinking about car racing-sometimes even watching it on TV- but as infrequently as is possible.

"Thomas, what's wrong?" Olivia snaps me back to reality, which is a good thing because the traffic is getting heavy as we approach Orlando, and Florida drivers are really terrible. The slick surface on the roadway doesn't help either. I am not sure if the problem motorist mayhem is caused by the advanced average age of Florida drivers in general, the fact that so many people have moved to the Sunshine state from other places, the number of tourists who are basically lost in search of the attractions, the perpetual construction of highways and bi-ways or the infiltration of basic rudeness into society. Heck, we have daily drive-by shootings and rolled over semis as well.

"Just trying to connect the dots. Josh is right, there's not much we can do without more information."

"True. Let's chill a bit. I got a bad feeling that we will be eating and sleeping this case for a while."

"I prefer eating eggs Benedict and sleeping with you," I respond, which gets me a punch in the arm-and then a quick kiss on the cheek lest my attention is diverted.

"You are really a dirty old man."

"At your service." Another punch.

"Just concentrate on the road smarty."

"I have a thought. Really. I want to check out each race in which Montgomery drove during the last year. Location, what he drove, qualifying and finishing positions and the names of other competitors. I want to see if there is a pattern. I can't see Cosmo bothering with a novice stock car driver. It just doesn't fit the image of a small time drug distributor. "

"After we check Montgomery's bank records, we may have more dots to connect," the beautiful Detective suggests. "I would love to take a look at Montgomery's computer, but I don't think we have sufficient cause to get a warrant."

"We have enough to keep us busy for a while. I am most anxious to get time a look inside Cosmo's computer. He must maintain some kind of ledger."

"Patience, my dear Thomas Ballard, journalist extraordinaire. Let's follow orders and relax for the rest of the day."

"What a remarkable suggestion, my dear Detective Nederfield. Your place or mine?"

"Who's got the bigger TV?"

"The question is who has the more comfortable bed?" Yup, I get another punch in the arm.

"I should probably clean my house today, but since I want to avoid feeling guilty, we will go to your house. Since it looks like we will be spending a few days at the beach, I want to make sure I have the proper clothing in the Airstream."

For those of you who may not remember, my home away from home, now our home away from home, is a classic, perfectly restored 1955 Airstream Flying Cloud travel trailer, which I use whenever I am required to spend an overnight out of Orlando-and it looks like Daytona may be our designated venue for several days.

Since I am a regular, I don't have to jump through hoops to get press credentials. Getting into Daytona Speedway as a journalist can be difficult if you are free lance, but inasmuch as my writing is featured in lots of on-line publications, plus an occasional print periodical, my bona fides are accepted pretty much everywhere. Needless to say, Olivia's badge opens doors everywhere.

I want to concentrate on driving. The VW is cute but a bit squeamish at 70 plus miles per hour. "Sweetie, I think that we had better find out how much our travel allowance will be before we go shopping."

"We may have to buy beer for some good old boys when we start asking around for information."

"Good point. This is definitely a beer rather than a Bordeaux kind of crowd. I'm going to miss the Bentley gang. They bring a certain kind of class to where ever they are."

"Maybe we can invite them?" I suggest.

"To a stock car race? Thomas, those folks are way too elegant."

"I'll bet they would enjoy it. I'll ask Josh to make them special deputies and get them onto the race."

"Slow down. I don't want them dragged into another murder investigation," Olivia answers.

"I don't want them dragged into anything. I am suggesting that we ask for their help. They are the best."

"I agree that their skills equal or exceed anyone's, but this is different than the other two cases we had with them."

Detective Nederfield is right, of course. It's that I feel that both my back and my front are covered when I am with the Bentley Seven. Maybe we'll invite them to another stock car race. I know they would have fun.

Being the considerate chap that I am, I have cleaned up my garage so that Olivia's VW can be housed inside. Well, so is my Airstream. My F-250 sits on the driveway.

"Thomas, why don't you leave my car out here until I have made sure everything we need is safely, neatly and properly stowed? How many days do you think we'll be at the track?"

"I think we should get there early Thursday and return after the feature event on Sunday late afternoon. I have no idea what we are looking for, so the more time, the better. Also the closer to the actual race, the harder it will be to get to talk to people. I always get my best interviews a couple of days before the race and hope to get a twenty second sound bite after the race."

"We're going to need a lot of supplies. We haven't had an extended stay in Nellie Belle for a couple of months."

"Nellie Belle?"

"I think the Airstream needs a name."

"It has a name . . . Airstream."

"It now has a new name . . . Nellie Belle."

CHAPTER SEVEN

Olivia wasn't kidding when she said that we needed to resupply Nellie Belle Airstream. After spending about an hour going through my trusty home away from home-making sure the generator was working and had plenty of fuel, filling the water tanks (I'm glad I emptied the waste tank when we got back from Georgia), checking the propane for the stove and refrigerator (I also have a real ice box on board) and otherwise making sure everything was tip top, I yield to Olivia. With practiced efficiency, she checks the linens, our clothes, including foul weather gear in case a storm comes rolling off the Atlantic, a reminder that hurricane season doesn't officially end until November.

"So much for relaxing," I say after checking tire pressure. "I bet Josh is sitting at home watching a football game. It's too wet to work in the yard."

"Your next assignment awaits," Olivia cheerfully announces. "Please tidy up, including wiping down every surface, both vertical and horizontal with the appropriate cleaner and making sure that we have an adequate supply of paper towels, toilet paper, dish soap, foil and wrap."

I wonder if I should salute. I suspect that would result in being on the receiving end of yet another punch in the arm. I nod in compliance.

"I think it is time for a glass of wine," Olivia finally announces.

I look at my watch. It's almost six. "Time flies when you're having fun." I smile at the grubby Detective Nederfield.

"Job well done, Special Deputy Ballard. I've made up a shopping list, including a six pack of . . . Dr. Pepper." She starts to laugh at our private joke.

"Lest you forget, we're out of here Thursday morning." Although the track at Daytona is only an hour or so away, traffic, especially on a race weekend, has made the journey a trek rather than a trip. At least we are getting V.I.P. treatment. Journalists are relegated to the back of the line, but law enforcement is given front row seat-figuratively speaking.

"Heads or tails?" Olivia asks.

"For what?" I respond.

"For getting to take first shower."

"We can save water and take a shower together," I suggest.

"I need to wash my hair. So let me make a suggestion."

I patiently wait. "And what might that be?'

"You open some wine and decide what to make for dinner. I'll be ready in fifteen minutes and promise to save you a little hot water." Olivia turns and walks toward the master suite.

Actually, the house only has two bedrooms: the so-called master bedroom with its own two sink bathroom, and a smaller room with a pull out couch which shares the second bathroom with the rest of the house. The kitchen is large, modern and gets a lot of use. Decisions, decisions. What to have for dinner. The day is turning into evening and the damp and dankness still lingers. What better than some clam chowder and a warm baguette of French bread which I will retrieve from the freezer, wrap in foil and slowly heat. The chowder is even easier-Tony's of Cedar Key makes the best clam chowder and has won so many awards it was banned from entering cook-offs. Mix a can equally with half and half, warm and voila. I select a chilled chardonnay from the wine cooler, ask Alexa to play Cole Porter and perfection has been achieved-except I still need to take a shower.

Armed with two glasses of wine, I approach the bathroom door which is slightly ajar. "Are you decent?" I ask.

"Since when did you start asking?"

Taking that as a yes, I enter. Olivia, at 6 foot 2, standing in front of the sink with a towel wrapped around her head and wearing my Ritz bathrobe, is breath taking. Rather than say something stupid, I hand her one of the glasses. "Cheers. Dinner will be ready in about fifteen minutes. May I use the shower?"

Olivia takes a sip from her glass and walks up to me. She forgets to fasten the robe. I am forgetting to breathe. "Later," she says and walks out.

Hot shower-cold shower? I can't decide. I take a sip. Hot shower and pray I won't need a cold shower after dinner. Nah! Suddenly the door opens. I am in my all togetherness. Unfazed, Olivia says, dinner smells terrific. And don't forget to wash behind your ears. I break into laughter. Definitely a hot shower.

Feeling scrubby-clean, I re-enter the kitchen. Olivia has set the table, lighted a candle which smells like pears and honey, put some olive oil and oregano in a dipping dish for the bread. "Ready?" She asks.

Rather than say *"for what?"* I simply pull back her chair and say, "Alexa, please turn down the music."

CHAPTER EIGHT

Once again I am shocked into reality by the obnoxious sound of an alarm-or is it the telephone? I turn over and reach for Olivia. The bed is empty, but the sound that awoke me is gone. A vision enters the master suite with my ritualistic cup of coffee. "Two guesses."

"Let me think. It was either a telemarketer or Chief McCarthy, right?"

"Deputy Ballard, your powers of deduction are unexcelled. Fearless leader wanted to tell us that Cosmo's phone has been found, somewhat worse for the wear. It appears that his killer attempted to destroy the phone by shooting it, but the tech guys think they can retrieve the data, including all his contacts, texts and possibly computer and email passwords. It may take a day. The Boss is really excited."

"Like 6:45 in the morning excited?" I reply.

"It could have been midnight instead. That's when they found the assassinated phone." Olivia starts to giggle. "I can visualize some hood standing over the cell phone and filling it full of lead. *Take that you lousy phone!*"

"You may sound like Edward G. Robinson, but you don't look a thing like him."

"Does he still expect us at ten?" I ask.

"Do you have something else in mind?"

I exercise great restraint and respond, "I want to check the NASCAR web site and compare the dates in the calendar to dates Montgomery raced, his finishing position and the amount of money the calendar seems to say he was paid. I hope that Josh will get the bank records first thing. We only have three days of office time before we leave."

"Since we over indulged ourselves at Betty's I thought a healthy breakfast is in order. Fresh blueberries and oatmeal with walnuts."

"Sounds perfect. I'm going to hop into the shower and then see if I can make any sense out of the connection between Costello and Montgomery."

"It may be nothing," Olivia suggests.

"Neither of us believes in coincidences, so there is a connection. Whether it has anything to do with the demise of Cosmo is still under investigation." I think that sounds somewhat erudite for a car guy.

"Do you need to warm up your coffee before you retire to the bathroom?"

"What a splendid idea, my darling." It's getting a little thick.

"Don't forget, we have to prepare an invoice for our trip. Knowing Sheriff McCarthy, anything in excess of cold cereal for breakfast, hot dogs and chips for lunch and pasta for dinner, washed down with a Dr. Pepper, will be considered extravagant."

"A motel room at Daytona Beach during race week, even at the skuzziest place will be $300 per night. So giving us each $200 a day is a super deal. Don't forget to add fuel.

Towing Nellie Belle consumes great volumes of fuel so we will add $1.50 per mile times 150 miles . . . another $225."

"And don't forget, we will need an entertainment fund for food and beverages required during the assignment. Maybe even a glass of wine for that special unexpected guest. "

"Bottom line . . . twelve hundred dollars." I give Olivia a *thumbs up* which she returns with a kiss. Well, an *air kiss*. I'm psyched. I will even sneak in time to write something pithy for my readers.

I must admit, oatmeal is good for the soul. A little cinnamon, nutmeg and 1% milk makes a man healthy, wealthy and wise-at least healthy. Searching the database for all the races in which Montgomery participated is easy. With the new digital lap time apps, I can also see his time for each lap of each race or practice session. All this is very cool, but also quite useless. There is no pattern. Nothing stands out. His lap times were consistent with his finishing position. This is important because if Montgomery was intending to throw a race, he would either have sandbagged from the start or suddenly slowed toward the end of the race. The data did not support this hypothesis. Also, his starting and finishing positions would show a trend. Basically, he finished near where he started-never at the back of the pack. Trying to manipulate grid position amongst a group of young and hungry drivers would be virtually impossible. I didn't find any correlation between finishing position and money purportedly paid by Costello. Big fat zero. I am bummed out.

"Any luck?" Olivia asks as she exits the master bedroom wearing light gray pants, medium blue blouse and a single strand of pearls which accentuates her detective badge hanging from a silver breakaway chain. The breakaway part is important in case some bad guy grabs you and tries to choke you with your own chain. I have one, too. Detective Nederfield's choice of footwear is definitely of the practical variety-dark gray Nike walking shoes. Her pocketbook is also of the practical variety and big enough to hold her weapon of the day, hand cuffs, wallet, lipstick, compact, mace and cell phone. What? No taser?

"I won't bore you with the details, but there are no dots to connect between Montgomery's performance at a race and the amount of money listed on the calendar. The data suggests only that the young driver performed well and with consistency at any given race."

Suddenly a shaft of sunlight pushes its way into the kitchen.

"Thomas . . . a sign." Olivia is being a bit tongue and cheek.

"Kind of like the Bat sign. Josh is calling us to headquarters."

"Let's take the VW. Maybe it will be nice enough to put down the top after our meeting."

CHAPTER NINE

At least there wasn't any hooting and hollering when we entered headquarters. Clothing, they say, makes the man or woman. My all business look-blue blazer, light green button down collar dress shirt, nicely pressed chinos and highly polished brown loafers-clearly set the tone. Like my gorgeous blond *partner*, I also wear my badge hanging from a breakaway chain.

"Good morning Detective Nederfield and Deputy Ballard. My, don't you two look spiffy."

Orange County Sheriff McCarthy can be hurtfully sarcastic. I think we look good, especially compared to the Sheriff who is wearing his ugly forest green uniform-with four stars on the collar.

Down to business. "Josh did you get Montgomery's bank records yet?"

"Yes and no."

"That's not an answer," Detective Nederfield correctly observes.

"The judge would only issue a limited search warrant because the connection between the calendar and Montgomery is a bit of a stretch. He did order the bank to compare deposits into the account with the dates and amounts set forth in the calendar and if they match, he will consider expanding the scope of the investigation."

Although Josh is disappointed he didn't get what he wanted, I think he appreciates that the judge was balancing the rights of someone whose connection to Costello's death is tenuous with law enforcement's need for all of Montgomery's records. This time I agree with the judge, like my opinion makes a difference.

"Well, Supreme One, what do the deposits records show?" I ask.

Sheriff McCarthy looks down at the floor and shuffles his feet the way a little kid does after being caught with his hand in the cookie jar. Suddenly, he pumps the air with his fist. "A perfect match! I am personally going before Judge Brewster and ask him for an omnibus search warrant regarding all of Montgomery's financial records."

"Including his computer and cell phone?" Olivia raises an interesting question.

"Yes, but I expect that my request will be somewhat limited. Judge Brewster is a very careful and cautious guy, so I believe he will want us to establish a stronger connection between Montgomery and the decedent. But if I get his transaction records from the bank, we should be able to follow the deposits."

"The old *follow the money* trick," I quip.

"Yup." Sheriff McCarthy is gloating.

"Thomas, on the way to the Courthouse, you can fill the Boss in on the matrix you developed regarding races in which Montgomery participated, his performance and the deposits from the calendar which we now know are accurate."

"Wait a minute! Why are you two coming with me?"

"One, because you might need to discuss something with us so that you are prepared to answer any questions that Judge Brewster might ask. Two, we will be the chief investigators on the case, having spent yesterday afternoon preparing for our surveillance at Daytona Beach."

"And thirdly," Olivia begins, "you like our company."

Josh speaks into the microphone on his shoulder walkie-talkie. "Helen, would you please bring down a copy of the calendar from the Costello case and the affidavit we received from the Palm Trust Bank regarding deposits into Donald Montgomery's account. Thanks."

"Shall we drive over in my car?" Olivia asks.

"And who is going to sit in the back Detective Nederfield?"

I hate it when Josh makes a good point because I'd be stuck in the back with my chin on my knees.

Sheriff McCarthy once again speaks into the shoulder microphone. "And Helen, would ask someone in the motor pool to bring around an unmarked Explorer. Detective Nederfield, Deputy Ballard and I are heading over to see Judge Brewster. Thanks."

Although one of the perks of the job would be a car and driver, Josh prefers low key. He drives himself to and from work in his own aging Jeep Wrangler, often in civvies and even sometimes on his restored 1947 Indian Scout. If he needs an official car he uses whatever is available.

Sheriff McCarthy's executive assistant is a retired dispatcher who worked the board for Orange County 911 for almost thirty years. She is battle tested and nothing, and I mean nothing, flusters her. Her appearance is amusing especially juxtaposed to Josh's bear-like physique. She is a hair above 5 foot tall and maybe weighs 100 pounds soaking wet. Her sparkling green eyes are both soothing and laser-like.

Helen Walker is extremely protective of the Boss with whom she has worked since he became Sheriff twelve years ago. Although in her mid sixties, she has neither reason nor inclination to let up. The McCarthy boys call her Aunt Helen and I call her Ma'am, although I have known the Sheriff for over four decades as my best friend.

With folder and keys in hand, we head out to our date with the judge.

Travel time to the Orange County Courthouse is only about twenty minutes from headquarters, including V.I.P. parking. When the *new* courthouse was built about twenty years ago, a lot of birds took up residence in the various nooks and crannies designed into the façade. An ornithologist, on jury duty after the opening of the building, identified the birds as crows. Inasmuch as a group of crows is called a *murder*, the local criminal defense lawyers immediately started a fund to collect money for the removal of the birds-without success.

Security at the courthouse is under the jurisdiction of the Sheriff's office, so when *the big cheese* arrives, we get a lot of immediate attention. After briefly explaining that we were there to see Judge Brewster, we are whisked through the metal detectors and escorted to the Judge's chambers on the third floor. A simple knock on the door results in coming face to face with a black robed man almost as big as Josh. Judge E. Cummings Brewster has been on the bench for sixteen years. Trial judges are elected in Florida, which to me raises a number of issues, but nevertheless, the voters got it right with Judge Brewster. Before coming to the bench, he was a public defender for eight years and before then was an offensive tackle for the New Orleans Saints while attending Tulane Law School.

"Please come in Sheriff McCarthy," he says in a deep baritone voice. "I assume your visit relates to the search warrant in the Costello case."

"Yes sir."

"What did you find?"

"The deposits into Mr. Montgomery's Palm Trust Bank account match the notations in the calendar. What we are seeking is a warrant to check all of Mr. Montgomery's financial records including his personal computer."

"A bit broad reaching, isn't it?"

"Yes and no. The bank is under an obligation to inform its client of the search warrant. They have given us a 24 hour hiatus." Josh is literally toe to toe with the Judge.

"I understand, but you haven't given me enough to give you that much access. I will give you a search warrant for all of Mr. Montgomery's financial records at Palm Trust Bank including any safe deposit box he may have and a 72 hour black out order regarding the bank notifying him. I want to connect the decedent to Montgomery more definitively."

"Your Honor, my name is Deputy Thomas Ballard and together with Detective Nederfield, we are the lead investigators in this matter." I can't keep my mouth shut.

"Aren't you a journalist who writes about car racing?" Judge Brewster asks incredulously.

"Yes, the same."

"Are you also a deputy sheriff?"

"Yes, your Honor. The department, under Sheriff McCarthy, has included a number of people with unique perspectives to join his office as special deputies. Since Mr. Montgomery is a race car driver, and since I have met with both him and the deceased while writing an article, I was asked to assist."

"I remember. You wrote a very in depth examination of gambling and car racing. Correct?"

"Yes, your Honor. After Sheriff McCarthy looked at the calendar, he concluded that car races in which Mr. Montgomery participated and what we have found to be payments to him, presumably made by Cosmo Costello, coincide. So we explored whether the payments to Mr. Montgomery reflect his performance in each race?"

"And what did you conclude Deputy Ballard?" Judge Brewster asks.

"After reviewing each race, including qualifying times, starting and finishing positions and lap times within each race for both Mr. Montgomery and his competition, I concluded that the amount of money he received did not relate to his performance."

"What were the payments for?" His Honor is following my presentation, for which I am relieved.

Josh resumes, "That is the $64,000 question. Thomas has all but eliminated gambling from the equation. While acknowledging that we are on a fishing expedition, a whole lot of smack is missing; there is no obvious connection between drugs and Montgomery."

"Josh, how much cocaine are we talking about?" Judge Brewster asks.

"Street value, over thirteen million dollars."

"Shit! Excuse me Detective Nederfield."

"Olivia, your Honor and we all agree that we have a problem on our hands. Not only this particular shipment, but without Cosmo Costello to keep peace, we may be confronting a changing of the guard that could lead to a drug turf war."

"I am still only giving you a limited search warrant, but I want to know what you find. Here is my cell number. Call if you can convince me to expand the parameters. How are you following up with Mr. Montgomery?"

"Your Honor, he is racing this weekend at Daytona and Detective Nederfield and I will be at the track, in my journalism persona, early Thursday. We are going to turn over as many stones as we can. Sheriff McCarthy will be arriving on Saturday and we will connect the many dots."

"Good. Sounds like you all have it under control. My clerk will have the search warrant typed up and signed in fifteen minutes. I will have her send it to the bank by email. I don't want them tipping your hand."

"Thanks Emil," Josh says.

"Giv'em hell, Josh." Judge Brewster turns and retreats to his office.

CHAPTER TEN

After picking up the search warrant from the Judge's clerk, we head back out of the Courthouse.

"Okay hot shot, what was that bit about hiring people with unique perspectives?" Josh is sounding a little testy.

"What should I have said? My mother used to feed the ever growing about to be sheriff with cookies after elementary school and as a thank you, he made me a special deputy."

"Good point, but what about me going to Daytona?"

"We will need a least one connect the dots meeting after you have hacked Costello's computer and analyzed Montgomery's bank records. Better the mountain come to Mohamed."

"You are a real pain in the butt Deputy Ballard, but we are not hacking Costello's computer. We are simply gaining lawful access. His cell phone, too."

"Stop it you two." Olivia claps her hands together-very reminiscent of my third grade teacher. Actually our third grade teacher. Josh and I do go way far back.

"Let's take the search warrant to the bank personally." Sheriff McCarthy can change the subject without batting an eye.

"Do you think they can give us the bank records right then and there?" Detective Nederfield asks.

"How limited are we?"

"Judge Brewster has given us a little flexibility. The bank should be able to retrieve electronically Montgomery's last three year's statements and email them while we are there. We can also find out whether he has any other accounts at Palm Trust Bank, including a safe deposit bank," Josh replies.

"And we are basically waiting until we can get into Costello's computer and cell phone," I quip.

"Yup." Josh curtly replies.

"Boss, has a thorough search of Costello's house been undertaken?" Olivia asks.

"Might be worth another look see as soon as we are done at the bank. Our team was basically searching for anything directly related to the murder. Let's concentrate on the bigger picture."

"Which is?" I am being a wise guy, in the literal sense.

"I'll let you know when I find it," Sheriff McCarthy jabs back.

"If you don't cut out this bantering I am going to send you both to detention." Principal Nederfield has spoken.

"Thomas, as I recall we've been sent there more than once." We both begin to laugh. It cuts the tension-not tension between us-but tension created by waiting for others to open a door we can walk through and investigate. I definitely think that we should see how good of a housekeeper Cosmo Costello was.

Although the Palm Trust Bank is only four blocks away from the Courthouse, we decide to drive the Explorer in case the bank gives us boxes of material or more likely because we are being lazy.

Faux Colonial era banks in Florida always amuse me. If a building is made of red brick with white Doric columns, is it safer or more efficient or more friendly than a modern glass and steel edifice? I guess some designer thinks so. The folks at the Palm Trust Bank are indeed friendly and efficient. Within a couple of minutes of entering the small private office of the branch manager, Marcus Whitman, according to a small sign on his desk, the financial records of Don Montgomery are flying through the ether to Josh's computer at headquarters. Mr. Whitman shuffles through some documents on his desk and shows us that young Montgomery also has is a safe deposit box at the bank. Unfortunately the box has to be drilled by a special locksmith which may take a day to accomplish. We are handed copies of the access log. Montgomery visits the box about once a month. We excuse ourselves from the tiny office. Speculation, here we come.

"Why would a young race car driver visit a safe deposit box each month?" I ask no one in particular.

"Could be to hide large amounts of cash he is regularly receiving." I can't fault Sheriff McCarthy's reasoning.

"I want to ask the bank manager to look up the name Cosmo Costello and see if he has any accounts here." Olivia says. Without waiting for a reply, Olivia re-enters the manager's office. We decide to look for the restroom.

We rendezvous in the lobby where we are surrounded by obvious copies of portraits of the Founding Fathers. It seems so incongruous with Central Florida, but a lot of people think that Disney World is also incongruous-located where orange groves stretched for as far as one could see and cattle crazed on tens of thousands of acres. A sigh for the good old days-outhouses, insects so prevalent that Orange

County was almost called Mosquito County and lest we forget-no internet.

"Jackpot!" Detective Nederfield is almost jumping up and down.

"Spill the beans," Josh commands.

"I convinced the charming bank manager that the search warrant included indentifying whether accounts at the bank funded Montgomery's account. He was a little hesitant because the big deposits were cash. I asked him point blank whether a Cosmo Costello had any relationship with the bank. I told him that he had been murdered two days ago and that I didn't want to waste the Judge's time asking for a search warrant if the decedent didn't have any accounts. A quick search of the bank's data base show that dear departed Cosmo had a checking account and a debit card. I tried to get the balance, but no luck. I asked if he had access to any other accounts. The sweet bank manager said he would have to do a significant data drop to see if Costello had any signature powers or had a POD on any accounts. But he said I could come back around closing and he should have the information." Olivia is all smiles.

"What's a POD?" Sheriff McCarthy asks.

"Payable on Death. It means who gets the money in your account when you die. It's a relatively new designation intended to make sure that money isn't hung up in probate forever. Olivia and I made each other POD's of our accounts a couple of weeks ago."

"That may be more information than I need to know."

"About PODs?"

"No, about the relationship between you two."

"I need a cup of coffee!" Olivia announces. "After I visit the ladies' room."

Josh and I break into gales of laughter. Olivia simply sticks out her tongue and walks away.

CHAPTER ELEVEN

To fill our caffeine deficiency, we return to headquarters. Despite what you've seen on TV, coffee at the Orange County Sheriff's office is about the best in town. When the new building was designed, Josh insisted that fresh coffee should always be available. I think he was tired of dirty pots, sloppy grounds and the smell of burned organic material in the air. Sheriff McCarthy had a number of these fabulous machines installed throughout the building, activated by scanning your ID. The user is offered a choice of six different coffees, three teas and hot chocolate. Each selection is freshly brewed in a clean cup. Real creamers and sweeteners are available in a variety of flavors. Visitors need to be actually visiting someone with an ID to get a cup of java. Also, *Big Brother* knows how much you have consumed in the course of a day and when.

Armed with steaming cups-two coffees and Earl Gray tea for me, we retreat into Josh's inner sanctum. Helen hands Sheriff McCarthy his phone messages received since we left. Each call is logged with the date, time, phone number and name of caller. Most law enforcement departments use a new data access system which allows them to identify the caller regardless of whether the ID is blocked or whether the call originated here or abroad or from a land line or a cell. So much for privacy. On the plus side, it certainly has reduced the number of people calling with threats.

"Anything that can't wait?" Josh asks his *major domo*.

"Calls relating to the Costello case are highlighted. I either forwarded routine calls or handled them myself. Your doctor called to remind you that you have a scheduled appointment tomorrow at 10. That's it."

"Did we get young Montgomery's bank records?"

"I downloaded them into his file and printed a copy of the statements." Helen hands the Sheriff a plain brown file folder.

"It appears that Cosmo Costello was a client of Palm Trust Bank. Please prepare an application for a search warrant and have someone walk it over to Judge Brewster. Detective Nederfield will serve the warrant later this afternoon on the sweet bank manager."

Ms Walker raises one eye brow, shakes her head and says, "I won't rise to the bait. I am sure the bank manager is sweet."

"Let's drink the coffee while it's hot, and Boss, I am not going to rise to the bait either," Detective Nederfield replies and then takes a huge gulp of java. "Much better."

Rather than saying something pithy, I simply start to laugh and almost spit up my precious cup of perfectly tepid Earl Gray tea.

"Let's go over Montgomery's bank records," I suggest. "I am still struggling with connecting the young driver to Cosmo. More importantly, finding a connection between Montgomery and Costello's business interests, which is what apparently caused his demise."

"Thomas is right," Olivia begins, "the dots do not connect."

"Yet." The always optimistic Sheriff of Orange County replies. "Drink up and let's see what we find."

We sit ourselves around a large conference table. Josh pushes a pile of annual bank statements toward each of us. The records include copies of all checks written during each monthly period and copies of all deposit slips. Mine is the most current pile which covers the last year. "I think we should all use the same accounting analysis," I suggest. "Let's list deposits by date and amount and source. Cash deposits will tell us nothing other than the date and amount. Before we list the checks issued from the account, let's create a numbering system. If the payee and service is obvious and recurring, we can . . ."

"You are making this very complicated," Josh says. "Instead of acting like this is an IRS audit, why don't we each review the year's documents we have and then share what we find."

"Thomas, would you like another cup of tea?" Olivia asks.

"Okay, I get it . . . keep it simple."

Both Olivia and Josh barely control an outbreak of laughter. I don't see what is so funny. I was just trying to keep us all on the same page. I pick up the January bank statement. "May I write on these?" I ask holding up a document.

"To your heart's content." Sheriff McCarthy's sarcasm is not lost on me. "Would colored markers help?"

"Actually, that would be very nice," I reply. I can be as snippy as the next guy.

"Any preferred color?"

"Would you two stop acting like children? We have a lot of questions and no answers. Start looking for them in bank statements." Detective Nederfield now sounds like a Sunday school teacher Josh and I had.

"Yes, ma'am!" Josh exclaims.

"Can I have my tea now?" I suspect if Olivia had poured the liquid, it would be dripping down my face.

I rise and walk over to Josh's king sized desk and take a yellow marker from a pencil holder, return to my seat and pick up the bank statement again. No one says a word. The only sound for the next hour is the rustling of paper.

A knock on the Sheriff's door awakens each of us from whatever. Before Josh replies, the door opens.

Helen enters and places several documents in front of Sheriff McCarthy and simply says, "Please sign here . . . here . . . and here. Judge Brewster's clerk is waiting downstairs. You are getting gold star service."

"Thank you. I suspect you had something to do with that." Josh says after scribbling his signature of the search warrant application and affidavit.

"It's why you pay me the big bucks. The clerk said she will have the judge sign the search warrant and get an intern to bring it back here so that Detective Nederfield can serve the sweet bank manager." Helen gives Olivia a most obvious wink.

"I declare a five minute bathroom and caffeine break," Josh says already heading out of his office.

"Find anything interesting?" I ask Olivia.

"The young man is very methodical. He puts a notation on the bottom of each check regarding the service for which he pays and more importantly notes each deposit with the name of person from whom he got the deposit and reason."

"I agree. He makes it easy. On each of the cash deposit slips he wrote the letters "ZC" and the deposits match the calendar entries. Let's wait for Josh. He will be insufferable if we solve the case before he gets back from the men's room." Olivia radiates a smile.

"I promised you a cup of tea, Thomas . . . and I always keep my promises." Lauren Bacall has nothing on Detective Olivia Nederfield.

The door slams open with a butt check from the Sheriff who is holding three cups. "Coffee for my hard working Detective; tea for my less hard working Special Deputy; and coffee for the Boss."

I am trying to make up a cool line to respond to Olivia's sultry comment, but fail. Later.

"Has anyone made any progress?" Chief McCarthy asks after gulping an entire cup of what appeared to be steaming coffee.

I raise my hand. He points at me.

"Each cash payment noted on Cosmo's calendar was deposited into young Montgomery's account. The amounts seem to correlate to expenses relating to the race car. For example, one entry had a deposit of $4,000 and the related car costs during that month were almost exactly the same amount. It looks like a budget for the season had been prepared and Costello paid Montgomery whatever was needed. I think it was a budget and not a reimbursement. The numbers line up. When the car was going to need tires or major mechanical work, it had been anticipated. A lot of young drivers are financially reactive and other than minor recurring things like fuel costs and oil changes, they never build in things like tires or a transmission rebuild."

"It makes sense. Remember the kid was an engineer. He costed out an entire season. He even had a reserve for unanticipated expenses. It was like Costello was sponsoring the kid." Sheriff McCarthy's analysis is spot on.

"Thomas, can you find out who sponsors Montgomery's race efforts?" Olivia asks.

"Unless he has a major seasonal sponsor, most young drivers get spot sponsors. Someone to pick up the tab for a race or two. No sponsor for a race . . . no race. It looks like Montgomery put together a full year race program and Costello funded it. I'll learn more at the track. People love talking about money. Mostly complaining about not having enough."

"We need to find Montgomery's budget to get a lock on Costello as the money man," Josh suggests.

"I think both you gentlemen have forgotten something," Olivia says.

She pauses, but we both know that she will tell us even if we don't ask, but I can't wait that long.

"What have we forgotten, insightful one?" I ask.

"This weekend's race. Has money been put into Montgomery's account today? It's Monday and he will have expenses. Without Cosmo, where is the funding?"

I have to admit that Olivia has made an excellent point.

"Detective Nederfield, when you serve the sweet bank manager, please ask him to check today's deposits to see if cash has gone into young Montgomery's account." Josh starts to stroke his chin, which he has done since we were kids, whenever he is deep in thought.

"Knock knock! I am not done with telling you about the bank records," I insert. Before anyone can say a thing I continue. "Every month our up and coming driver receives a deposit in the amount of three thousand dollars from the Tessa Family Trust, which is automatically deposited and which he uses for regular living expenses like rent, utilities and insurance."

"I noticed that from last year's statements as well," Olivia says.

"There were Tessa Trust deposits from three years ago, but they only began in September," Josh adds.

"Another dot to connect." This is certainly no less confusing than it was earlier in the day. I want to spend a little more time reviewing the statements and maybe Olivia's and Josh's as well. We really need to get into Cosmo's computer.

CHAPTER TWELVE

I have found that the best path to take when one reaches a fork in the road is the one that leads to the money. With apologies to Robert Frost, following the money usually leads to suspects or at least clues that lead to suspects. I am struggling to see how the money trail between Costello and Montgomery has anything to do with the former's death, although the question that lingers is: why is a gangster sponsoring a young driver's race car?

"Time for lunch," Josh announces. "It's almost 1o'clock. Houlihan's?"

Houlihan's is a pub frequented by cops. It is modeled after the kind of place you see in movies; Irish theme, dark wood, long bar with brass railings, always busy as people move on and off shifts, and friendly. There is a dart game in progress 24/7 and the food is really good and cheap. For years it was a male bastion, but now it is a cop bastion without gender distinction. Occasionally a member of the fourth estate working the crime beat frequents Houlihan's, as I did first starting out. Since I am a hybrid, half law enforcement and half journalist, entering with Josh and Olivia confers credibility upon me. Although I am not really hungry and a beer would put me to sleep, somehow the place inspires crime solving.

"Good day to Orange County's finest," the bartender purrs in brogue.

"And good day to you, Sean," Sheriff McCarthy brogues in reply. "Three half pints of Harp. We're still on duty."

"Lunch?" The Bartender asks.

Josh looks at Olivia who signs *just a little.* I nod. "Three cups of your darling mother's stew."

"May I say how ravishing you look today Detective Nederfield?"

"You may . . . anytime." Olivia's smile lights up the room.

"And I see that the press is hanging around."

"May I quote you?" I quip.

"Provided you spell my name correctly. How are you doing Thomas?"

"Other than hanging around this guy, I'm fine."

"You guys go way too far back. Grab the table in the corner and I'll bring the libations."

"Good choice of places to eat, Josh." I give him *thumbs up.*

"It's family. Remember when my dad brought us here? We were about ten and they served us a short lager and lime." Sheriff McCarthy's father was Chief of Police for the City of Orlando.

Being a cop is in his blood.

"We thought we were hot stuff."

"It's wonderful to reminisce, boys, but we have no real leads on a rather nasty homicide." Detective Nederfield brings reality into our 'working' lunch.

"When do you think we will have access to Cosmos' computer and cell?" I ask.

"I'll call Helen and have her track down the geek squad. We need to connect some dots, not simply find more," Josh answers. He retrieves his cell from his pocket and dials. The phone rings four times and is picked up by voice mail. Josh hangs up. "That's strange. Helen never leaves the office when I'm out."

In the background we here, "He's over in the corner hiding from you. Are you joining them for lunch?"

Seconds later Helen appears. "I wish you would turn the ringer volume on the highest setting. I've been trying to reach you for about fifteen minutes. The IT section called and they have accessed the computer and are going through it now. Apparently Mr. Costello was reasonably tech savvy because most of his files are layer password protected. Simply said, you need two different passwords for each file. I scheduled you three to meet with the technicians in their conference room in about an hour. The cell phone is still a work in progress."

"Care to join us?" It's really the only thing the Sheriff can say.

"Yes. Thank you. I am a bit hungry."

No sooner said than done. Sean approaches with a tray upon which four half pints of amber beer are resting. "I ordered you a cup of stew Helen. Does that meet with your approval?"

"Indeed it does, Sean. Say hello to your sweet mother for me." Helen replies.

"Talking about sweet, has the search warrant been issued?"

My silly comment is met with a swift kick in the ankles. I think Olivia is over the *sweet* joke.

"Signed, sealed, and about to be delivered," Helen responds.

"While the wheels of justice carry on without us for an hour . . . cheers." I lift my mug. The others follow.

"Boss, has there been any street chatter about Cosmos' death?" Olivia asks.

"Nothing that I have heard. Strange. Sean, do you have a minute?" Chief McCarthy bellows.

A brief side note. Sean Dooley, our bartender, is a retired state police homicide investigator and is totally wired into the stories behind the story.

"You summonsed me?" His blue eyes sparkle.

"Anything on the street about Cosmo Costello?"

"He has been keeping a pretty tight lid on the *undesirables.* Thanks be. Cosmo is not a regular, as you can imagine. He keeps to himself. Sorry Sheriff . . . nothing. Let me get your stew." Sean turns and bustles back to the kitchen.

"Humpf!" While not the most eloquent word, it certainly conveys our collective feelings.

"Do you think they are circling the wagons? It has been 48 hours since Costello was killed." Olivia raises a good point.

"Maybe there are no wagons to circle. Maybe it was a private hit. A *vendetta.* Unauthorized and done by a lone coyote," I offer.

"That is going to make the investigation more difficult especially if the Montgomery connection goes nowhere." Helen has clearly been involved in law enforcement for years.

"Let's eat and think in silence. Better for the digestion." Detective Nederfield says as Sean returns with four steaming cups of the best Irish stew west of Dublin, including Boston.

Although Houlihan's is packed, the ambient noise is relatively subdued. If the patrons are eating, there is no need to say a word. Just enjoy.

Sean returns to clear away our empty cups and mugs. "Sheriff, shall I enquire about Mr. Costello?"

"Very subtly," Josh replies. "Let others raise the subject."

"If I hear anything of interest, I will call Helen." Clearly the bartender knows the chain of command.

"Thanks and tell your mom that the stew tastes even better than it smells."

"Coming from a McCarthy, big praise." Sean Dooley winks and whisks away dishes.

CHAPTER THIRTEEN

Helen, Olivia and I leave and quickly walk the two blocks back to headquarters. Josh remains behind, not only to pay the bill, which he insists on doing, but also to chat with Sean about Costello. The less anyone knows, the better.

"What time do you want to get to the bank?" I turn to Olivia.

"I think I should be there before three so that I can get Costello's records and maybe examine Montgomery's safe deposit box."

"Don't forget to ask about any cash deposits into his account."

"Fear not Thomas, Wonder Woman is on the job." Olivia and Helen both laugh. I simply hold open the door to the Orange County Sheriff's sparkling new building.

"Doorman, please hold it for me," a somewhat breathless and red faced Josh McCarthy calls.

"By all means." I hold out my hand, palm up. Instead of a tip, which I richly deserve, I get a *low five.* So much for service.

We join the ladies and take the elevator to the fourth floor. The Operations Center is to the right and Josh's office is to the left.

"I will bring the search warrant to you as soon as it arrives," Helen says to Olivia, ignoring the two of us.

"Thanks." Detective Nederfield replies.

I am tempted to link arms and skip down the corridor singing *we are off to see the wizard,* but I stifle the urge.

"Does the geek squad ever leave the building?" I ask.

"Why would they? They are fed in the cafeteria, sleep at their desks and play video games all day long." Josh looks at us for a reaction. None is forthcoming.

An advantage of being the big cheese is that you can walk into any office without knocking. Despite all the ridicule the IT folks are subject to, their offices look like a swarm of activity. No video games in sight.

"Sheriff McCarthy, my name is Francis Dick and I am the head of this section. Would you join me in the conference room? We have had some success in accessing the data on decedent's computer, but have not yet deciphered the encrypted messages in his email account. Mr. Costello was quite creative in building security into his system. Everything is stored on a private server and each account requires two passwords for access. He also installed a doomsday safety feature. If you fail to enter either password correctly after two attempts, the account is frozen. We have had to be very careful, but have been rather successful."

"I am very pleased." Josh seems at a loss for words.

"However," the chief geek continues, "I think you will be disappointed at what we found. Hopefully, the encrypted messages, all of which were sent from an account, amato02903@gmail.com, will be viewable shortly."

"Let's take a look at what you were able to unlock." Josh is getting impatient.

"The deceased used a number of ordinary applications, eBay, PayPal, Netflix, Amazon and Etsy. We analyzed the last twelve months and found that everything looked normal."

I can't resist. "What's normal?"

"Purchases and payments matched. For example, if Mr. Costello bought something on eBay, he paid for it by using PayPal. If he sold something on Etsy, the purchase price was sent to his PayPal account."

"Like how much are we talking about . . . this buying and selling?" Out Sheriff is not happy.

"About $1,000 a month in purchases and $1,000 in sales."

"Mr. Dick, is there a pattern to what Mr. Costello bought and sold?" Olivia is definitely trying to be calm and collected and patient, unlike her two companions.

"Most definitely Detective, the deceased seems to have an interest in old books which he buys and sometimes sells. I studied a couple of transaction and in one case he bought the same book twice, but then sold one copy. I am assuming he retained the better edition. His purchases from Amazon were more straightforward."

"How so?" I ask. This is like pulling teeth.

"Oh . . . well . . . he purchased some personal items like underwear and a pair of fleece lined slippers. Let' see, he bought a microwave . . ."

"Enough! Mr. Dick, thank you for your diligence, but this is a murder investigation and you are employed by the Sheriff of Orange County . . . me. Did you find anything that might assist us in that task?"

"No, Sir. Even his Netflix account is benign. There is nothing out of the ordinary, except his layered security system and encryption."

"You seem to have resolved the first issue, what is the timetable for opening the encrypted email account?" I think that is a reasonable question.

"And the cell phone?" Olivia adds.

The diminutive and bespeckled geek shrugs.

"Detective Nederfield . . . Deputy Ballard, I think we are done here. Mr. Dick, please put as many resources as are needed on cracking Costello's cipher and retrieving data from his cell . . . and call my office immediately with anything useful." Sheriff McCarthy emphasizes the word useful.

Following Josh's lead, we exit the conference room and then the larger den of nerds.

"Now that was interesting," I adroitly observe.

"How so?" Olivia picks up that I am trying to calm down our fearless leader.

"Seems like Cosmo Costello was just your average American."

"You mean the kind that distributes drugs and probably has had a number of people killed."

"Ah yes, that kind of average American," I answer.

"Let's see what the sweet banker has for Detective Nederfield, who is expected to return to headquarters immediately after getting the warrant served."

"You mean I won't be able to join Mr. Whitman for a drink after the bank closes?"

"Only after you get Costello's bank records, check whether cash was deposited into Montgomery's account today, find out if Costello has a connection to any other account at the bank and get the contents of Montgomery's safe deposit box . . . all by four o'clock."

"Can I add my two cents?"

Olivia and Josh both shout, "No!" We all start to laugh.

CHAPTER FOURTEEN

"Thomas, your brow is furrowed. What's up?" Olivia asks.

"I just had a thought," I answer.

"That explains the furrowed brow. It happens so infrequently." Sheriff McCarthy has a real mean streak.

"I wonder if Costello's email address has any significance . . . amato 02903."

"Amato means beloved or sweetness in Italian," Olivia says.

"02903 looks like a zip code," Josh adds.

I stop to look at my phone's screen. After typing in a few commands, I say, "No surprise. 02903 is the zip code for a part of Providence known as Federal Hill."

"Mob central," our esteemed Sheriff replies.

"It's logical as an email address. I don't see any meaningful relevance, but nevertheless a good thought Thomas." Olivia is trying to make me feel better.

"I hope Helen has the search warrant. It's almost three o'clock." Before Josh opens his office door, Helen appears with the aforementioned warrant.

"Detective Nederfield, I have a car waiting outside to take you to the bank with instructions to wait and bring you back here," Helen says. I am curious if she knew about Olivia's plans to have a drink with the sweet bank manager. Best to keep your thoughts to yourself.

"Thank you," Olivia replies to the proffered document. "See you all real soon." She turns and sashays down the hall.

Josh just shakes his head. Me, too.

"Sheriff, if I can get your attention for a minute, there are several other cases in the office which require your attention." Helen is clearly in charge. "And Deputy Ballard, you got a call from the Volusia Sheriff's office about this weekend. You can use the back office."

It suddenly occurred to me that I need a hook to get in tight with Don Montgomery. Up close and personal is the only way we are going to be able to determine whether Costello's patronage of his racing efforts is in any way connected to Cosmos' death and the missing drugs. If the contents of the safe deposit box don't give us some serious insight, it is going to be a long weekend.

After phoning both the Sheriff's office in neighboring Volusia County and the PR folks at the track, I begin to put together a requisition form for expenses which I decide to give directly to Helen, bypassing my cheap friend.

Olivia returns in less than an hour. So much for drinks. Followed by Josh, they enter my temporary office. "We got or are getting everything from the bank . . . more or less." she announces.

"I'm more interested in the got than the getting." I hope no one takes offense.

"I got the sweet manager to send over Costello's bank statements including his debit card. He does not have a safe deposit box, but . . . drum roll . . . he opened and made the initial deposit to the Tessa Family Trust account two and one half years ago. Six thousand dollars is deposited into the account from a bank in Providence every month and then three thousand is put into young Montgomery's account. The bad news is that Montgomery's safe deposit box won't be opened until late tomorrow. The locksmith is out sick."

"See what happens if you don't get your flu shot, you screw up a murder investigation." My mirth is not really appreciated.

"Trying to find a meaningful and relevant connection between Costello and Montgomery is enough of a pain, now we've got to figure out the connection with the Tessa Family Trust . . . and Providence. Where does the other three thousand dollars go?" Sheriff McCarthy is an unhappy camper. "Helen, can you reschedule my doctor's appointment," he bellows.

"No!" She answers. "You have postponed it three times and Cheryl and I have said your health is more important than solving the murder of someone the world is better off without anyway."

"Josh, Olivia and I will look at Costello's bank statements and debit charges tomorrow morning, although I bet that there is nothing of any interest. Anything of significance would most likely be paid in cash. What I want to spend my time on until we get into Montgomery's safe deposit box is writing and posting a piece on a couple of up and coming drivers competing at the greatest race venue in the world. Actually, it will be more like a teaser promoting an article on which I will be doing research this weekend."

"You are actually smarter than you look." McCarthy can be so complimentary.

"Thank you great one. We try."

"Well done Thomas." Helen enters the now crowded office with a folder. "The bank records of one Cosmo Costello, recently deceased." She hands the folder to Olivia. "Enjoy."

Helen Walker is formal when there is a likelihood of someone overhearing, but in the privacy of the Boss' office, she is everyone's Aunt Helen.

"In order to make this credible, we need to take our leave, so that I can get to know the up and coming as opposed to the rich and famous," I suggest. "And you can rescue the rest of Orange County. Oh by the way Helen, here is our expense requisition form for the weekend." I hand the pink sheet to her.

"Let me see that!" Josh shouts.

Helen playfully slaps his wrist. "Let's get back to work."

It's hard not to laugh-so we do. Even the mean old Sheriff smiles.

We turn to leave when Olivia suddenly says, "I forget to tell you, the bank does not show any deposit into Montgomery's account today, however any deposit after 2 p.m. won't be posted until tonight and won't show up in his account until tomorrow. The sweet Mr. Whitman will call me in the morning. I will ask again about the safe deposit box."

"May I make a suggestion?" I ask.

"Since when did you ever ask?" Josh replies.

"Since I think you need yet another search warrant. This time for the bank records of Tessa Family Trust." I smile as opposed to smirk.

"Do you think that Judge Brewster is going to get tired of us running back and forth?" Olivia asks.

"Actually, no. Judge Brewster likes to take things slow and easy. By submitting applications at each juncture as evidence evolves, we keep him in the loop. I suspect that there may be a time in this case where we may have to ask him to go out on a limb and I want to have a solid track record."

"It's too late now to visit the sweet bank manager. He's probably having a drink by now anyway. You are out 'til noon with the doctors . . ."

"I hope not!"

"Whatever. I am going to need most of the day to put together and circulate my article and we also need to go through Costello's bank records and hopefully Tessa Family Trust records as well."

"Montgomery's safe deposit box may be ready," Olivia wishfully says.

"Let's keep in touch by phone," Josh adds.

"Please keep the ringer on high." I quickly move to the door before my dearest and oldest friend hits me.

CHAPTER FIFTEEN

"I'm beat. Let's go to the 709 for a glass of wine and some soup," I propose.

"I second that!" Olivia replies.

We lower the top of the VW, exit the parking structure and aim the trusty steed toward one of our favorite *known only to locals* eateries. Nestled in an upscale neighborhood, the 709 is a former Ma and Pa corner store now converted into a very low key wine and beer hangout with an outstanding light fare. We usually walk the three blocks, but since we are already in the car and dog tired, from what I am not exactly sure, driving seems like a good idea.

"I want to take a hot shower when we get home and read something that is not a bank record." Detective Nederfield's façade is crumbling.

Mine too. "I think a clean start on the morrow is a great plan. I am going to hide both the land line phone and both our cells until 8 o'clock. If the mean ogre calls, we will tell him we went for a ten mile jog."

Olivia starts to giggle. "Someday we should ask him to accompany us. Did you see him after lunch? I thought he was going to pass out." Giggle becomes laughter.

"Before Daytona opens for real business on Saturday morning, they have a charity run around the track. It's only a 5K. I think we should enter and somehow get Josh to join us."

"I agree with the former but unless there is a table of Krispy Crème donuts at the finish line, the latter is unlikely. Actually, we should get up and put in some miles. It's been three days."

"I agree, but can we wait until 7ish?" I am a wimp and proud of it.

"Up and out the door at 7:30 . . . deal?"

"I knew there is a reason I love you."

"What? Only one?" I get the not unexpected punch in my arm followed by a kiss on the cheek. And we haven't even had a glass of wine.

"You take first shower," Olivia shouts on our return to my house. "I want to check for messages. Regardless of what the big cheese thinks, I also have a couple of other cases I had better monitor.

"I'll be quick," I cheerfully reply. I also need some time in my computer. I also want to see what I can find on the NASCAR driver's profile page about Don Montgomery and select a couple of comparable young competitors.

I am nagged by the thought that we are too focused on the Costello-Montgomery relationship. Let's assume the cash Costello is depositing for the race car is generated from illegal activities, what does that have to do with his death? I think that he was killed because of the cocaine- now missing. Could the deal have gone wrong? Did Costello show up expecting to pay for the smack, but the delivery guys seized the opportunity to keep both? I can't believe that we are looking at an ordered hit. Maybe a faction wanted to move in on Cosmo's territory. Once again, I can't believe it was authorized. Are we talking about dissatisfied insiders or disenfranchised outsiders? Shit, I wish I knew more about the intricacies of this business. Actually, I don't want to know more. I am a car guy. That's all. Occasionally I lend my skill set, albeit limited, to solve some kind of nastiness.

My dialogue with myself is interrupted by a kiss on the neck generated by a sweet smelling woman. "You okay?"

"Now I am. I was just trying to put another spin on things . . . without real success. Everything surviving without you at the office?"

"Couple of drive-by shootings, a domestic homicide, and a *stand your ground* shooting in conjunction with a home invasion . . . you know the usual. I forgot . . . and this may be important, two suspected drug couriers were found with their throats cut in Miami-Dade."

"They weren't, by chance, carrying some cocaine for delivery to one Cosmo Costello?"

"Hard to tell. It took the coroner the better part of a week to put the victims together to identify."

"Sounds like a rather nasty M.O." I am more convinced than ever that the car connection is a red herring. This is something much different.

"I am going to make some hot chocolate. Want some?" Olivia purrs.

"Then bed time?"

"Then sleep time. We have a very full day tomorrow and likely so for the next couple of days."

"Party pooper." I maturely stick out my tongue.

"Don't forget about the extra vacation time Sheriff McCarthy gave us."

"He hasn't given me anything except grief."

"My, isn't the race car journalist a bit touchy?"

"No . . . just frustrated."

"Come on, it hasn't been that long."

"Silly girl. I mean nothing fits together. Cosmo's death is no further being resolved than it was ten minutes after you identified the body."

After a big hug and kiss, Olivia says, "We promised to sleep on it. I'll set the alarm."

CHAPTER SIXTEEN

We walk, run and jog about eight miles before we call it a fulfilling routine. I don't hurt nearly as much as I thought I would.

"Thomas . . ." Olivia says in between taking in large amounts of fresh air, "I think we should do this at least four times a week."

"I've got something else in mind we should do at least four times a week." I quickly move away to avoid the inevitable punch from the lovely Detective Nederfield.

"Let's shower and have something nutritious for breakfast." I think Olivia is too tired to hit me.

"Fried eggs, bacon and white bread doesn't seem to be on the menu," I reply.

"But granola with slivered almonds, 1% milk and black coffee for me and tea for you is featured at Chez Ballard."

"I'll flip you for first shower."

No sooner than my words were uttered, Olivia sprints to the front door and says, "Heads I win, tails you lose. You can make me a cup of steaming java."

The only way to begin a story or an article is to-start. In my case, I start with some preliminary research about the new crop of potential All-Stars emerging form racing's minor leagues. I actually cheat a little by including only drivers who are scheduled to race this weekend at Daytona. Since this piece is only intended as an entré to some of the younger drivers, specifically Don Montgomery, I am a bit liberal with facts and flexible on attribution of sources. Lest I forget, I have a real story or two to write and post about the race itself.

"I'm heading down to headquarters. I reviewed all of Costello's bank and debit card statements. Boring. Three thousand dollars is deposited into his account every month from Tessa Family Trust. He uses the account to pay his bills. Nothing out of the ordinary. Even his debit card payments are unremarkable. PayPal deducts from his account the amounts the geeks told us about. He does not have a mortgage payment, pays his real estate taxes and insurances by e-check, and otherwise lives within his monthly budget."

"Just like Montgomery." I add.

"Yup. I wish we could get a hold of the records of the account that makes the deposit into the Tessa Family Trust."

"Fat chance, the account is in Rhode Island."

"Unless we get the Feds involved."

"The missing cocaine?" I ask.

"Yup. But we are going to have to find the drugs or tie them to Costello's murder."

"What about the murder of the couriers?" I ask.

"That's why I am going to the office. I want to talk with the lead investigators in Miami-Dade. Maybe the Feds are already involved. After the Coast Guard followed the cocaine to Miami, they passed the assignment to DEA. They were to track the shipment. I don't subscribe to *the poof it's gone* theory. Did the couriers give the DEA a slip or did the DEA screw up?"

"Darling, don't get yourself into a swivet. Our job is to find out who killed Cosmo."

"Actually, our job is a great deal more than that. Josh doesn't really care who killed Costello. Good riddens. He is worried about a turf war to fill the void and millions of dollars of smack which may be headed here.

"Touché! I was thinking myopically. I still think that the maxim *follow the money* is the soundest way to proceed. I'll focus on Montgomery-Costello and you focus on the disappearing coke and compare notes later this afternoon after I finish my homework."

"Hopefully, I will get into Montgomery's safe deposit box. Thomas, neither of us believes in coincidences, so I keep thinking that the driver, mobster and the missing drugs are all tied together."

"I agree . . . and Olivia . . . I love you." For that I get a big smooch.

"I will get our well deserved expense check from Helen and pick up basic non perishable supplies on the way home, where you no doubtedly will have a wonderful dinner prepared."

"Sounds like everything is well planned. I have total discretion regarding tonight's menu?"

"Provided you plan, prepare and clean up . . . absolute discretion."

"In that case, I want to wish you the very best of success in your investigative duties in which you engage during the balance of the day."

"Thomas, can you ever say something in a couple of words?"

"Yes my dear . . . good luck."

"I love you too."

"Parting is such sweet sorrow."

"Good bye Deputy Ballard." Olivia grabs her oversized handbag and leaves.

"Farewell Detective Nederfield." I blow a kiss. She laughs.

Looks like I have a lot of work ahead of me. First, I need to make a list of potential young drivers for my article and then learn something about each and then write something cleaver and catchy which will make my approach to Mr. Montgomery easier. Time to make another cup of tea while my computer boots up.

CHAPTER SEVENTEEN

The table is set and the scent of Tiki Masala, which is simmering on the stove-chicken, peppers, onions and a rich Indian tomato sauce, wafts through the house. I will add some *right out of the garden*, sliced in half, super sweet cherry tomatoes, when I serve the dish over rice. A Shiraz is opened, waiting to be poured as soon as Olivia returns.

"Wow! Something smells terrific. I am starved." Olivia is carrying three shopping bags in addition to her ubiquitous giant purse.

"Can I help?"

"Thomas, be a dear and put these bags into Nellie Belle. Don't put anything away. I just don't want more clutter in the house than absolutely necessary."

I complete my rather simple task and return to find or rather hear Olivia in the shower. Being of a chivalrous nature, I knock before entering, although not waiting for an answer. "Hard day?" I ask.

"Big time. I'll be out in a minute. Shiriz will be fine. Actually, maybe a short Maker's Mark with a single ice cube."

"Wow! You must have had a hard day. Jeeves, the bartender at your service." I thought about hanging around until Olivia got out of the shower, but that may not be well received. It's all about timing.

The weather is Chamber of Commerce perfect and I raise the patio umbrella, wipe off the table and chairs, place two glasses of amber liquid thereupon and retrieve some Triscuits from the panty and brie from the refrigerator. I do this in record time since Olivia decides to forego drying her hair and wraps it in a large red terry cloth towel instead.

"I feel 100% better," Olivia says, sipping from her glass. "Cheers! Maybe I'll let you stay at home and prepare dinner every night."

"Hey, I worked too. The article has been launched into the ether and I have already gotten quite a bit of feedback, which leads me to the subject of logistics. I think we need to leave for the track tomorrow noon rather than Thursday. A media *meet and greet* has been scheduled for 5 o'clock and I have already RSVP'd for us. It establishes your bona fides as a journalist immediately without explaining who you are all weekend. Asking questions as a reporter is fine, but asking questions as a cop is not."

"You have been busy, Thomas and I love you." Olivia gives me a Kentucky bourbon kiss. "I bought almost everything we will need, except some basic perishables like milk and eggs. Also, we will need to stop at the package store for beer and wine."

"An absolute necessity." I raise my glass. "So tell me about your day."

"I struck out at the bank. The sweet manager was out sick today. His executive assistant said that the locksmith had drilled the box but she wasn't authorized to release the contents to me. I explained that the search warrant did not afford her that option whereupon she broke into tears saying she'd be fired if she acted on her own accord. She said that if Mr. Whitman is still sick tomorrow, she would get another branch manager to give me access. I told her that I would return at 10 in the morning with a deputy to seize the box if necessary.

"Am I to assume that deputy is me?"

"You are so astute it sometime takes my breath away."

"I thought that was my charm and good looks."

"That, too."

"Any progress on Cosmos' phone or encryption?"

"Nothing to write home about. The geek squad is still working. Josh even called Tyler Nelson for help."

"Ouch! That must have hurt. But I guess it was inevitable that the FBI would be on scene soon."

"I must admit that the Boss was coy. He told Nelson that his chief IT was out with the flu and he needed an expert to work on some encrypted files connected with a murder. Simple local jurisdiction stuff, but he reminded Agent Nelson how the Sheriff's office had provided an underwater search and rescue team when a stolen armored vehicle drove into a rather nasty alligator filled lake. I guess the FBI boys didn't want to get their nicely pressed suits wet."

"Nor, as I recall, were the Feds real eager to get up close and personal with a 'gator." We both start to giggle. "Welcome to Florida, land of sunshine, orange groves and bad ass mean prehistoric reptiles."

"I am hoping we will have something juicy from the cell and computer soon, but timing is uncertain."

See what I mean about timing. It's everything.

"What else has you upset?" I ask.

"It's just that everyday people are doing bad things to other people, many of them innocent bystanders. I know it is inherent in the job, but I am not investigating. I am not trying to solve murders. We know who the shooter is and usually why he or she shot the victim. We usually have the suspect in custody within hours of the incident. What gets to me is the underlying reasons for the violence. Often it's petty drug deals, but just as often it is something like *they didn't give me respect* or *their car cut me off* or *their dog pooped in my yard.* Since it sometimes seems that everyone in Orange County has a gun, it's much easier to simply shoot the offending party, who may or may not shoot back."

There is nothing I can say so I get up and walk over to my beautiful partner and give her the biggest bear hug I can muster. I am rewarded with a kiss.

"The Cosmo Costello murder is different. It has substantial ramifications and you will be investigating and trying to solve his murder which might lead us to the solving the murder of the couriers and recovery of enough coke to kill a lot of people. It is what you signed on for and are very good at."

I hook my arm into hers and lead her to the patio.

CHAPTER EIGHTEEN

After receiving rave reviews on dinner, I clean and put away the dishes. It's a two pan meal; one for rice and one for everything else. Olivia hands me a list which includes: beer (two cases), wine (six bottles) and Dr. Pepper (two six packs-don't ask). "We need to get all this tomorrow morning at the package store. I want to get milk, instant oatmeal, a couple of limes, a dozen eggs, a package of turkey bacon and some fruit. That should hold us, especially if we end up going to a couple of dreadful race track buffets. I do agree with you that down and dirty Saturday night oval track racing has the best food."

"If you like hot dogs and hamburgers."

"You men are so in the dark. For about three months, we girls have replaced meat with turkey. You slugs are eating lean turkey burgers and turkey hot dogs and can't tell the difference."

"Since when have you become one of the girls?"

"Since you have been dragging me to tracks every Wednesday, Thursday and Friday, with an occasional weekend race thrown in if the big boys aren't competing."

"Do I sense dissatisfaction?"

"I didn't say that. In fact I rather enjoy the escape from law enforcement and most of the women are down to earth."

"Do they know you are a cop?"

"Yes . . . and so do their husbands. Keeps domestic tranquility at a high level."

"You are really something special."

"And don't you dare forget it." Olivia emphasizes her point with a kiss.

"Since we have to be at the bank at 10, we need to rise early. I just put all the stuff you bought into Nellie Belle, like you said." I can't believe I just called my trusty Airstream *Nellie Belle.*

"I want to get in a fast paced three miles in the morning and then I'll sort everything out. We still need to pack. Thomas . . . thanks for dinner and thanks for being you. It was a tough day." This time I get a hug to go with the kiss.

I love it when I get a chance to ditz Sheriff Josh. Olivia and I are up and out so early, his 6:30 call arrives after we have done our morning workout and after we have showered, dressed and packed for the weekend. "Good morning fearless leader. To what do I owe this call?" I sound entirely too chipper for the curmudgeon. "Wait! Let me put you on speaker so that Olivia can hear."

"Hi Boss." We both note a sound that sounds like a grunt.

"I got a note from Helen that she gave you a check. I didn't authorize it."

"Josh, go take a cold shower and call back later. We have things to do including getting ready to leave today rather than tomorrow and we have a meeting with the bank at 10 o'clock."

"Why today?" Sheriff McCarthy sputters.

"Because there is media meet and greet with the drivers at five this afternoon and it will validate Olivia's cover. Anything else? Have you gotten into Costello's encrypted account or his phone. You may be the Sheriff, but let us do our job." Olivia looks at me and suddenly signals a *thumbs up*.

"You are mighty cranky this morning. All I was going to ask is *do you have enough advance money for the weekend?"*

"I don't believe you for a minute, but you are still my best friend, present company excluded."

"As it should be. Remember my doctor's appointment yesterday? Well he's scheduled me for a cardio workup; EGK, echogram and stress test all day starting in about two hours . . . and no food or caffeine. I think he also wants me to lose a few pounds."

"How many few?" I ask as delicately as possible.

"Like thirty."

"Ouch. We have everything pretty much under control on our end. There is plenty to be done and I suspect there will be more when the geek team is finished. Take care and be a good boy and follow the doctor's orders. I do not want to run for Sheriff of Orange County. If you are up to it, try to get over to the track. Bring your boys. They'll love it and so will Cheryl having all the testosterone out of the house for a few hours. Let me know and I'll get tickets put aside."

"Thanks Thomas. Deputy Nederfield . . . keep an eye on him."

"Will do Boss. I will keep Helen in the loop. And don't worry; you need a heart to have cardio problems."

"You guys know how to kick someone when he's down. Good hunting." Josh disconnects the call.

"Not good. The weight is one thing; the stress of the job is another." Olivia's concern is deep felt.

"We'll just have to cover for him."

"Thomas, the department has a lot of very capable and hard working members. But Josh is the glue and the spirit."

"He'll be fine. I hope we get the Costello case off his plate. I think he is worried sick about a drug war here in Orlando."

"We've got our work cut out for us with nothing really to go on."

"Yup. That's why we get paid the big bucks."

Olivia starts to laugh.

"Go put our clothes in Nellie Belle . . . neatly."

"Yes, your detectiveship."

"You are crazy as they come, but I do love you. Now go!"

CHAPTER NINETEEN

Fortunately I have developed a system for hooking up the Airstream to my truck. Olivia has stored all our groceries and I even placed my clothes on hangers as needed. It looks like home. The bank is only about fifteen minutes away and in our practiced efficiency, it is only 9 o'clock.

I suggest, "I think we should get the beer and wine now. It'll be easier to park this early in the morning."

"Good idea. I'm ready. Let's go to the liquor store on State Street. We need ice and they sell both block and cubes."

Although my Airstream has a real refrigerator, it also has a real ice box into which the aforementioned block of ice will be placed. It works fantastically well and will keep beer, Dr. Pepper and wine cold for about five days without more ice.

Since Olivia wants to make a statement at the bank, we are each wearing our Sheriff looking civvies; chinos and a white collared shirt. I even wear socks for the occasion. Our badges hang from a chain. I prefer not to carry a gun. When asked I reply *the pen is mightier than the sword.* Several rookie deputies think that I have a James Bond-like pen that fires who knows what. Olivia keeps her weapon in her massive purse, unless we are really going somewhere dangerous in which event she carries an issue 9mm Glock on a service belt. Since I am a deputy, albeit a special deputy, I am required to take firearm training and practice at least once a month. Olivia has always maintained a high proficiency standard, so I join her weekly and have achieved a certain level of accuracy myself. My weapon of choice is old school-a .38 five shot chrome Police special shortie. If I am absolutely required to bear arms, usually to cover Olivia, I keep my gun in a jacket pocket with my hand gripping the revolver entirely too tightly. I usually select an old jacket to wear in case I have to fire through the pocket.

Upon entering the bank, we are greeted by the sweet bank manager. Since the last time he and I met, I was in the company of the Orange County Sheriff and Sheriff's Detective Nederfield, my presence simply reinforces Olivia's suggestion to Mr. Whitman's assistant that one way or another we are not leaving without the contents of Montgomery's safe deposit box.

"Good morning . . . good morning. I want to apologize, but I came down with a bug the other day and was literally flat on my back yesterday. I know you are in a hurry so let's go the vault area and retrieve the box. I have the bank key and the other lock has been drilled."

"Thank you Mr. Whitman. We are in a bit of a rush since Judge Brewster is awaiting our call." I think that an occasional zinger is appropriate. It works. The sweet bank manager appears somewhat paler than he did a few minutes ago. Maybe a recurrence of his recent illness.

We are ushered into the inner sanctum of the bank. Mr. Whitman retrieves the box and places it in front of us and with a flourish, inserts the key and unlocks Don Montgomery's safe deposit box, at long last. Olivia and I both peer into the metal container and then at each other. Detective Nederfield retrieves a pair of latex gloves from her purse and removes several packets of paper and a large stack of United States Treasury Bonds, Bills and Notes. Rather than examine the contents in front of the rather nosy bank manager, Olivia places the papers into a large evidence bag. She seals the bag and writes today's date and time on the plastic.

"Thank you for your cooperation, Mr. Whitman," Olivia says rising to her full height. The banker is speechless. We turn and retrace our steps.

"Cool move, my dear," I whisper as we exit the bank building. "I think we should have left Nellie Belle at home. Parking at headquarters, where I assume we are heading, may be difficult."

Olivia removes her cell phone and speeds dials. "Helen, can you call impound and ask them to make a space so that Thomas and I can park the truck and trailer. We coming from the bank with the contents from Mr. Montgomery's safe deposit bank and then leaving for Daytona." Olivia pauses to listen to Helen's reply. "Thanks."

"Good plan, Detective Nederfield."

"Carry on, Deputy Ballard."

While the distance between the bank and headquarters is close as the bird flies, Orlando is experiencing so much building that birds don't fly anywhere near headquarters. Although I seldom use the perks of the job, I decide to place my battery powered, magnetic blue light on the roof of the truck. Not that anyone cares, but it makes me feel like I am doing something important and in a hurry since we really need to be on the road in an hour. The boys in blue, or in the case of the Sheriff's Department, boys in green, have cleared away a space big enough for a 747.

"I guess a call from the Boss' office carries a lot of weight." I pull up toward the rear entrance."

"How long do you expect to be?" A young deputy asks.

"About an hour," Olivia answers.

"Shall I have your rig turned around so that it is easier and quicker to leave?"

"Yes please," I reply. "Keys are in the ignition."

"My name is Deputy Karen McGinnis, so call down right before you are ready to leave."

"Thank you deputy," Olivia answers, as we abandon Nellie Belle to a stranger.

"First stop, the crime lab, I assume," I say.

"You are beginning to think like a cop," Olivia chides me.

"Heaven forbid." I shake my head in feigned disgust.

The crime lab is on the third floor. As we enter, it is obvious that we are expected. Helen, no doubt.

"Anything other than fingerprints?" The technician asks.

"I know you have Costello's prints but do you have Don Montgomery's fingerprints?" Olivia wants to make this quick.

"Yes ma'am. He has a concealed weapons permit and after we got a call from the Sheriff's office giving us the heads up, we pulled the permit and made sure we had scanned images of both individuals."

"Helen," Olivia and I whisper simultaneously.

"Also, is it possible to find out where the bonds came from?"

"Do you mean where the bonds were issued or who purchased the bonds?"

"Both but that can wait until later. We are interested in looking at the stacks of documents. Can you give us a place to work? After you check for prints, we need to look at the papers."

"Is this table okay?" The technician already has several gloved assistants beginning the identification process.

"Perfect," Olivia answers.

The technical process moves quickly. We are the slow ones. Many of the documents are rather basic: diplomas from elementary, middle and high school as well as Sunday school. I assume his college diploma is hanging on his wall at home. His baptismal certificate lists his name as Dominic. It also lists his parent's names; Giovanni and Teresa Pasatti, as well as the name of his Godfather; Cosmo Costello. After glancing at a number of otherwise irrelevant papers, we see a *Live Birth Certificate* listing his parents, including his mother's maiden name; Costello, his place of birth; Providence, Rhode Island. Giovanni Pasatti is listed as having been born in Palermo, Sicily. Several dots connected. The lab guys are working hard, but we simply do not have time to wait.

"Have you been able to ID any prints?" Detective Nederfield asks the crime lab technician.

"There are a lot of partials and smudges. The only clear prints are those of Don Montgomery. We still have to go over this other stack of papers and the bonds. We are working as fast as we can."

"We understand and we appreciate the efforts you all are making. Here is our problem: we need to leave; we need to examine the documents and we need to know the identification of the prints." I think I am being succinct.

"I can call you when we are done and you can pick up everything. I can have it waiting at the front desk." The technician is trying to be helpful.

"Except that we are leaving for Daytona in ten minutes." Olivia is also without an answer.

"Excuse me," a young lab person says. "I live in Ormond Beach and could drop off everything on my way home tonight. Just tell me where to go."

"That's perfect. Will you be done by then?" I ask.

"For the fingerprints, for sure. I am not sure about the treasury instruments. There are about forty. Getting the prints, no problem. Getting the place of purchase shouldn't be a problem. But getting the name of the purchaser depends in large part on when the instruments were bought. Everything sold by the Fed in the last ten years is on a single data base. Before, the information was kept by the Federal Reserve Bank in which the bond, note or T-bill was sold. If they were all sold in the same district, it is a lot easier."

"Get us the documents and instruments after you've done the print check and as soon as you have the purchase info, email your findings to me and copy the Sheriff. We are going to be at the Daytona Raceway. Do you know where that is?"

"Oh yes. How cool."

"Here is my cell number. Call when you get to the Main Gate. I will alert security. And what is your name?" Olivia says.

"My name is Eleanor Price. I am an intern. I am studying law at Stetson."

"Thank you Eleanor Price. You are really being a big help."

"Are you a fan of racing?" I ask. Always the journalist.

"Oh yes. My dad used to race at New Smyrna and I was his pit crew."

"I will make arrangements for two tickets for both Saturday's and Sunday's feature events."

"Oh wow. Thanks sooo much."

"Thank you all." Olivia and I leave and head upstairs to talk to Helen who may have an update on Josh's tests.

CHAPTER TWENTY

Deputy McGinnis has the truck and Nellie Belle ready to rock and roll. "I had one of the mechanics check your tire pressure and take a look at the tow hitch and wiring and he pronounced everything was in tip top shape. I thank her, but knew that all systems were fine since I spent the better part of Sunday checking it out myself.

"Thank you Deputy McGinnis for your attention to detail." Coming from a detective and a woman, I think that the young officer was pleased. Also an extra pair of eyes is always a good thing.

The hardest part of our journey to the track is the first three or four miles, bobbing and weaving around orange traffic cones and other construction barriers in our attempt to get on I-4, one of the worst roads in America. Once we are free from the so-called ultimate roadway project, even with towing the Airstream, we are at the Media gate in about an hour. Now registering and getting parked is entirely different. Daytona is the crown jewel of race tracks, not just here in Florida, but probably in the world. A massive amount of money was invested in the facility and it really is state-of-the-art.

Sheriff McCarthy's clout and my not insignificant recognition as a motor racing journalist snags us a great parking space-and it's only 3 o'clock. Time enough to get settled and prepared. I don't even know what the race program looks like. There will be practice and qualifying tomorrow for all groups and then a little of everything on Friday culminating in the 250 mile roval feature for the big boys on Sunday.

"Thomas, did you know that they are having two 50 lap races for vintage stock cars on the oval on both Friday and Saturday afternoon?"

"That should be a hoot. Those were the days. Half the drivers were still running moonshine. The imagery of the unwieldy steel monsters driving three abreast toward the waving checkered flag is awe inspiring. Bumping and shoving one another. Their names say it all: Smokey, Fireball, Junior, Tiny, Freddie, Buck, and Speedy. They drove Pontiac, Oldsmobile, Plymouth, Hudson, Ford, Buick, Mercury and Dodge."

"And they were lucky the mortality rate was as low as it was. No roll cages, proper seat belts, full face helmets, HANS, fire proof driver suits . . . blah, blah, blah."

"Since when did you become such an expert?"

"Since I started reading all your articles." Olivia takes my breath away.

Our visit down memory lane is interrupted by a knock on Nellie Belle's door.

"Who knows we are here?" I ask to anyone who is listening which I guess eliminates everyone except Olivia, who shrugs.

I open the door. I feel a surge of adrenalin. My heart starts to race.

"*Buongiorno,* Thomas."

"Who is it?" Olivia asks.

"Signorina Olivia. *Come stai?*"

"Franco, what are you doing here?" I recover from the shock.

"Senora Margarite wants to make sure you join us for dinner tonight after your meeting and greeting. She was very insistent." Franco shrugs his shoulders, but smiles in the way only an Italian can do.

"We mean, what are you doing at the track?" Olivia asks.

"Cecil is racing his Hudson Hornet and we all decided to come and watch." So much for not inviting the Bentley Seven to a stock car race.

"Who is Cecil?" I ask Franco.

"He is Charles' younger brother. He was several years behind us and became, how you say, a computer nerd. He invented a lot of things, which I don't understand, and has helped us for years. He taught Hans everything he knows . . . about computers. Anyway, he fell in love with what you call stock cars. Over the years he has purchased and restored several. He is racing a how do you say, Favoloso Hudson Hornet this weekend. I will let you unpack. Shall I tell Margarite to expect you for dinner?"

"Franco, where and when?" Olivia asks.

"*Mio Dio,* I forgot. We have two motor coaches. Very large since there are eight of us plus the car. All the old race cars and trailers are parked together at the yellow garages. They expect a lot of spectators to visit our area so they have a stand where the cars can be viewed. Very nice. See you later for dinner. I have got to get back and help Stanford prepare." With that, he leaves.

"Did what I think happen, actually happen?" I ask.

"I can't believe it. How could they know we would be here?"

"That part is somewhat understandable. It is one of the biggest races . . . anywhere. What scares me is that they are here and we are in the middle or actually the beginning of a murder investigation. I don't think that we should raise the subject. Agreed?"

"Agreed, but futile. Remember, the Bentley Seven is the most astute group of people we have ever met. They are wired to everyone and everything. Thomas, let's just stick with our game plan and see what happens."

"We really don't have much choice. Here's the bright side. We have our Bentley blazers and sweaters in the closet."

"Irony or intent?"

"Your call. I wonder what's on the menu."

"Since the track has fabulous facilities, I think you should go out and take a shower and change. We want to be on time and it's already almost four."

"You mean we don't have time for a nap?"

"Make that a cold shower."

CHAPTER TWENTY-ONE

Armed with my notes regarding the young drivers about whom I just wrote, the entry list for all the races, a small tape recorder (old fashioned mini cassette), a spiral notebook, several pens and my assistant, Olivia Nederfield, we leave for the reception. At least I hope they are serving something wet and cold, preferably draft beer. We have donned our basic Bentley informal attire: gray flannel pants, white shirt or blouse, a British green tie (pearls for Olivia) and matching blue blazers with stylized B on the front pocket. Hardly the stock car ensemble, but we do turn heads.

Several drivers, owners, crew chiefs, tire changers and other reporters come by to pay their respects. I think most of them want to be introduced to my gorgeous blonde partner. It is amazing how well Olivia adapts to her surroundings. Having spent the last few months absorbed in the car world, when she is not fighting crime, she has accumulated not only text book knowledge, but real life knowledge of the racing community. It doesn't hurt that she grew up with an internationally respected German car mechanic father, and also completely restored her VW bug from the ground up.

"I spy over yonder a bar which looks like it is serving beer. Care to join me?" I ask.

"I think that would be a splendid idea. I'll lead." Crowds seem to part like the Red Sea when Olivia crosses a crowded room.

"I think that is Don Montgomery standing next to Henry Fuller."

"Fuller has a couple of well financed cars in the Trophy series, correct?"

"Your wealth of information never ceases to amaze me. Young driver chatting with big time owner, smart move. Let's take a slight detour."

"Let's wait until we get a beer and then take a detour. I'm parched." Olivia always keeps her priorities in order.

The line is long, but moves swiftly. This crowd cannot be denied liquid refreshment of the alcoholic sort for any length of time. I try to surreptitiously glance at my notebook in which I have pasted pictures of the up and coming drivers. Montgomery is a match, and so is Louis Chapman standing next to another young driver, Ken Holtzman. Only one to go-Juan Carlos Cidado. I lean over toward Olivia and show her the photographs. She follows my eyes as I locate the young men.

"No women?"

"Alas, this year's crop of new stock car drivers does not have any women, but it does have one Argentinean."

"Who is very cute. I'll interview him." I get an elbow in the ribs.

"Keep your mind on why we are here Detective Nederfield. To detect."

"Let's go over and introduce ourselves to Don Montgomery." Olivia grabs my hand and drags me toward our unsuspecting target.

Before we get within ten feet of the pair, Henry Fuller shouts out, "Thomas Ballard, how are you? Now I know the guest list is complete."

"Henry it is always a pleasure to be in the presence of a true patron of the sport . . . provided you are winning." My sarcasm confuses both Olivia and young Montgomery, but Henry and I go way back-like before he was a gazillionare.

"But isn't that the point? Winning. And you being the bard of auto racing once said that there is little difference between second place and last place in the annuls of history."

"I am flattered you remembered. How are you doing, Henry?"

"Better, Thomas, and thanks for asking. But enough of us old farts; I would like you to meet Don Montgomery, who I think has a bright future in our sport and hopefully in my stable."

"I agree. I did a pre-race piece yesterday on the next generation and included a brief review of Mr. Montgomery's accomplishments."

"It's Don . . . and I saw the article. Thanks Mr. Ballard."

"It's Thomas . . . and I am quite impressed with your consistency and the care you take of your equipment."

"As an engineer, I appreciate the machine I drive and as an independent with only my uncle's help, I appreciate the cost if I break something."

"Are you from a racing family?" Olivia asks.

Before Montgomery can answer, Henry Fuller says, "Thomas . . . manners my boy . . . manners. You have failed to introduce me to this vision of beauty."

Olivia draws herself to her full 6'2' height, which is increased by modest heels, extends her hand and says, "Olivia Nederfield."

Henry's mouth is open but not closing.

"Ms. Nederfield is a Mercedes factory authorized performance test driver, as well as a contributor to numerous European magazines and is my sidekick at some of our more prestigious events."

"Well done Thomas. My apologies, Miss Nederfield. Our journalist friend has been to so many events alone, that people had begun to talk. Now he is with not only a ravishing beauty, but a gear head." Henry smiles from ear to ear showing a set of unnaturally white teeth.

I am thinking about a way to extract myself from this conversation without losing the chance to talk to Montgomery. Grab the bull by the horns. "Don, I would like to set up a time to interview you in depth over the weekend. What is your schedule?"

"Wow! I have non-qualifying practice at 9, so I should be done by about 11."

"Let's meet at my trailer. I am in the media parking section next to the red garages and have a classic Airstream."

"And I want to chat with young Montgomery on a more formal basis as well," Henry Fuller adds.

"Better get an agent," I quip.

"No problem. My Uncle Cosmo is a very savvy businessman and he reviews everything I do. I expect he'll be here Friday or Saturday morning. He never misses watching me race."

The kid is clueless. Let him stay that way for as long as possible.

"If you can fit in a few minutes after Mr. Ballard interrogates you, I'll meet you at noon at the driver's lounge," Henry adds and turns to go. "And farewell Miss Nederfield. And you too, Thomas."

"I better go and hook up with a couple of the guys before they think I'm a snob. See you a little before 11," young Montgomery says.

"Good luck tomorrow." I wish there was a racing equivalent of *break a leg.*

"This is going to be awkward." Olivia says.

"I don't relish breaking the news. He seems like a nice kid." I reply.

"What's Henry Fuller's story? He seems a bit full of himself. I think he's creepy, especially referring to Montgomery as possibly *joining his stable."*

"Your powers of observation are only exceeded by your beauty. Henry Fuller was a moderately successful lower tier stock car driver about twenty years ago. His style was more conducive to demolition derbies than stock cars. Some colorful altercations took place after Fuller pushed other drivers into walls. We would bump into one another at small venues up and down the East Coast. Okay guy to share one beer with, but not a second. He never struck me as the type with either ambition or a lot of gray matter. He stopped driving after a rather nasty crash which put him in the hospital and which race organizers considered egregious enough to suspend him for a year. I heard through the grapevine that he then got involved in a software company in California and developed several algorithms with tons of applications. His career choice certainly surprised the heck out of me, because Henry couldn't balance a check book. Best to him, although there were rumors that the processes weren't his and that the money was from a source not disclosed. Re-enter Henry as a wealthy team owner with factory help putting two cars on the track every weekend of the season. He always has one or two young drivers in training . . . in his stable.

"We had better touch base with the other drivers on your list so that we don't blow our cover." Olivia is right, as usual.

CHAPTER TWENTY-TWO

Juan Carlos Cidado is surrounded by a bevy of adoring admirers; men and women. Not bad for a guy who has never raced in a Trophy series event. I think I may have to do a bit more research into the young man's background. Not only does he look like he just walked out of a fashion magazine, but he is animated and certainly entertaining those around him.

"Let me handle Juan Carlos," Olivia whispers.

I nod. Like what else am I supposed to do?

Detective Nederfield quickly closes on the group. "Hola Juan Carlos." The crowd immediately is silenced.

"Hola Senorita . . ."

"Olivia."

"Buena noches."

"Y tu."

At this point, I am not sure where the conversation is headed, except that Juan Carlos is oozing every bit of charm he can. Considering Olivia is about six inches taller than the young driver, it is amusing to watch him try to get positioned. I decide to make an entrance. Extending my hand, I say, "Good evening, I'm Thomas Ballard."

"The famous writer, no?"

"The writer, yes. Famous, no."

"But you are. In Buenos Aires, you are read by everyone who is interested in motor racing, which is everyone." He laughs.

"Thank you. I want to spend a few minutes with you in the next few days for an interview," I suggest.

"Gracias. That would be very wonderful. I saw your article about the four new drivers and I would very much like to tell you my story. I think it makes me different from the others. You see, my father owns one of the largest ranches on the Pampas, but he did not like me wasting my time racing cars so he told me to . . . how do you say . . . get it out of my system and then come back home. He gives me nothing. My abuela, my grandmother, sends me enough for me to eat and sleep in a clean, safe place, but she agrees with my papa. I was fortunate to have had sponsors in South America, but it is more difficult here. Much more difficult."

Juan Carlos' entourage is beginning to get restless. "When do you have some free time tomorrow?" I ask.

"I have been working with Team Fuller and will practice with the Trophy cars tomorrow. If I do well, I will get to qualify."

"I will meet you at the driver's lounge at one o'clock. Okay?" Juan Carlos has some difficulty saying things in short sentences. I want to avoid running into Henry Fuller, also.

"Okay."

Olivia puts her arm through mine and directs me away from the Pampas Prince. "I need another beer after a few minutes with Juan Carlos." I say.

"I need to take a shower. He is way too slick. For someone on a grandmother's allowance he dresses like he is best friends with Armani," Olivia replies.

"I noticed. Rolex watch, heavy gold chain and his ring has an emerald the size of a golf ball. I didn't realize you spoke Spanish."

"Try being a cop in Orange County and not speak Spanish." We both chuckle and proceed post haste to the bar.

Our chats with Holtzman and Chapman are less than inspiring. Both are nice kids, but dull as dishwater. I avoid scheduling follow-up sessions. I feel slightly guilty, but a cold beer and being next to Detective Nederfield cures the pangs.

"There are a group of drivers over to the right who look interesting," Olivia observes.

The clutch of people are older, far better attired and speak without yelling at one another. I really didn't say *clutch* at a reception for car people, did I? We weave our way through the crowd.

When one says *that the apple doesn't fall far from the tree,* they were obviously talking about a family tree. In the middle of this distinguished group is the spitting image of Stanford, blazer and all. "I guess we found Cecil," I whisper to Olivia.

"They look like identical twins."

From behind us I hear a familiar voice: Margarite Leiter. "Olivia . . . Thomas, I am so glad to see you. Franco said he delivered our dinner invitation, but I wanted to make sure you two were rescued from hundreds of adoring fans. And I want you to meet Charles' brother, Cecil. You two look tres elegant this evening."

Margarite puts her arm in mine and leads us toward Cecil and his friends. The crowd steps aside as we approach and then re-forms behind us. "There is no question who is in charge," Olivia whispers. "Madam Leiter is the classiest person I have ever met."

I simply nod. One would not think that stock car racers, albeit vintage stock racers would be in her sphere of friends. Wrong. She is comfortable everywhere and with everyone. She puts people at ease with her charm, knowledge and attentiveness to others. Margarite Leiter defines all aspects of the world in which we wished we lived.

In her typical style, Margarite raises her hand and commands silence. "I would like you all to meet, Olivia and Thomas. They are dear friends of ours and will soon become dear friends of yours. Please introduce yourselves for I will probably mispronounce your names in my terrible English."

Margarite releases my arm and walks over to Cecil to whom she offers her hand, which he kisses. "Cecil, I would like you to greet Olivia and Thomas," Margarite continues.

"It is a pleasure to meet such a vision of loveliness and such an esteemed member of the fourth estate." Cecil even sounds like Charles.

"It is our pleasure," Olivia responds. "I am anxious for you to tell me all about how you were diverted from Bentleys to a good old American Hudson."

"With pleasure. Where shall I begin?"

"At dinner you silly goose, before it gets cold and Stanford throws it at you." Margarite is in rare form. *"Dépêchez-vous* . . . hurry up or we will be late for dinner." Margarite is addressing the entire crowd. She turns and with Cecil in tow, starts to march us two by two back to the yellow garages . . . and a fantastic dinner.

CHAPTER TWENTY-THREE

Being dressed in Bentley informal certainly helps us mingle with the crowd of about thirty vintage stock car devotees. We are clearly the youngest ones present which does wonders for a forty year plus ego. In addition to blazers as the garment of choice, several drivers are wearing sweaters with their team names embroidered over their hearts. The cars on display are remarkable. Considering that half the cars have suffered significant race damage over the years, each has been authentically restored, without regard for cost. Cecil's Hudson Hornet shows all the attention to detail that the Bentley gang puts into all their cars. It is way beyond cool, but so is the bevy of beautiful Buicks, the pod of sleek Pontiacs, the phalanx of fast Fords and the swarm of Studebakers (well actually only one). Chevrolet, Oldsmobile, Plymouth, Mercury and Dodge are also well represented. This is an aspect of automotive racing history that I am glad has finally gotten the recognition it deserves. Unlike vintage sports car racing, the old time drivers of these thundering steeds tend not to appear at events. I think that the phenomenon relates to the origin of the sport itself. Sports cars have always seemed aloof and exclusionary, reserved for the wealthy. Stock car racing, with its moonshine origins, is a part of the Southern fabric. It is the sport of the good ol' boys. Old stock cars were not preserved at the same rate as sports cars and were involved in far more wrecks. If a stock car was smashed beyond repair, the owner/driver would cannibalize anything salvageable and put it into another car. The sports car crowd believed in keeping the damaged vehicle intact. If a car sustained significant sheet metal damage, the car would be re-bodied. Sports cars were rare, while potential stock car racers were being driven to the market every day. Enough history especially since I see Franco rushing over to us with two glasses of wine.

"Signorina Olivia, Signore Thomas, some wine?" Franco must have run from culinary headquarters which I smell but can't see.

"Grazie," Olivia responds.

"Come see our kitchen." Franco offers Olivia his arm and the two head off toward the plume of smoke I see.

"Unbelievable!" I say to no one in particular. As we approach the area where all the teams have parked their trailers, actually rigs, since all are tractor/trailers, our senses are overwhelmed by the smell of sizzling meats; brisket, pork, chicken. Stanford, wearing a denim apron and a chef's hat, flanked by two assistants, is standing in front of several large metal smokers, waving a long fork. He reminds me of an orchestra conductor.

"Howdy!" Coming from a Welshman, his choice of words takes me back.

Without hesitation, Olivia answers back, "Howdy to you Stanford. Everything smells fantastic. Where did you learn to smoke country style?"

"When in Rome . . . We we'll catch up later. Bubba, Mary Sue and I have to feed a whole army. Franco, can you get me some more of the hickory wood from around back?"

"Si." Franco replies and turns to us. "He is beginning to refer to the kitchen as a chuck wagon. Please mingle."

"If I wrote a book about these folks, it would be listed as fiction. No one will believe me."

"So write it as fiction. Who cares if people believe the story? It's too good to be true anyway."

"Detective Nederfield, you are brilliant and beautiful." Never miss an opportunity to compliment the one you love. "Shall we mingle?"

"Saluti!" We clink glasses, which are real glass not cheap plastic. No big surprise.

"Bon jour *mes amis!*" Pierre, Margarite's brother and bon vivant, greets us-with a kiss on each cheek.

"Bon jour, Pierre. *Comment ça va?*" I reply.

"I do not complain since no one will listen to me anyway." Pierre smiles and shrugs.

We nod, greet and occasionally shake hands with the crowd as we wend our way to the area where all the cars entered in the exhibition races and a few more from the Daytona Museum are on display. I mutter to myself, *you've come a long ways baby.* The collection of steel and rubber conjure up images of days gone by. No carbon fiber, no colorful wraps, no self adjusting suspension, just simple back woods drivers man-handling thousands of pounds of steel at terrifying speeds, especially considering the tires and safety equipment or lack thereof.

"Ah, Olivia and Thomas . . . at last." Hans Leiter, Margarite's husband and the unspoken leader of the Bentley Seven or is it eight if we add Cecil?

We are welcomed with the kind of panache only culture and confidence brings. The remaining members of the group surround us; Charles, photographer extraordinaire, and Frederick, whose taciturn nature belies his mechanical abilities.

"And you have met Cecil, no?" Pierre says in a way only a Frenchman can turn a statement into a question.

"Your sister dragged us away just as Cecil was about to tell us the story of why he is driving a Hudson Hornet instead of a 4 ½ liter blower Bentley." I reply.

"I think the lovely Margarite was rescuing her guests from . . . me." Cecil chuckles at his own quip. "The Hudson Hornet was extremely technologically advanced for a car manufactured by a very small company with limited resources. It had a lower center of gravity and was lighter in weight than the other competitors. It has superb handling qualities and is so much fun to drive. Besides, everyone else had a Bentley and if you want to make a statement . . . *drive a Hudson.* Maybe you can enjoy a couple of laps on the Speedway."

"I know I would enjoy that," Olivia quickly replies.

"Me, too," I demurely add.

"Done. Be here about 7:30 tomorrow morning. We have an open, no passing practice session for V.I.Ps and other guests. And you two are my guests." Cecil is beaming with pride. Is it because he will be chauffeuring a world famous writer in his Fabulous Hudson Hornet or more likely because a beautiful blonde will be on board?

The presentation of these classic fire eating monsters is shortened by Stanford's announcement that *dinner is served.* I erroneously assumed that we would be eating country style-standing in small groups, balancing a paper plate full of food in one hand and a beer in another. You can take the chef out of the kitchen but you can't take the kitchen out of the chef. Four ten foot round tables, with enough room for dozens to eat in comfort at pre-set place settings, beckons. Franco and Stanford have placed flower arrangements in the center of each table attended by wait staff in matching white jackets. I notice that there are several younger apprentice crew members who have been recruited as part of their initiation into the racing fraternity. So much for equating stock car racing with hot dogs, hamburgers and beer. The aforementioned smoked meats are served with prerequisite baked beans, collard greens and corn bread. I am not going to ask how this feast was accomplished.

"Gathered friends," Hans says to the assembled after a few clinks on his raised wine glass. "We wish each of you a rewarding, entertaining but safe race weekend. A special thanks to chef Stanford, sommelier Franco and their wonderful crew, who will be changing tires, pouring petrol and otherwise keeping their drivers and their cars in perfect condition throughout the event. Cheers!"

A chorus of cheers, cin cins, santés, skolls and prosts greet our host. Rising with her hand raised, which immediately silences everyone, Margarite says, "Let us begin before this wonderful feast gets cold."

For the next half hour all you hear is the fork and knife upon plate, with an occasional *please pass* . . . I believe this is the closest to barbecue heaven I will ever get.

CHAPTER TWENTY-FOUR

My pocket begins to vibrate. I have a love-hate relationship with my cell phone. "Ballard here," I brusquely answer. I pause. "Oh great! Thank you Eleanor. Are you there now? Put the person at the gate on the phone." Olivia nods in acknowledgement. "Hi, this is Thomas Ballard. Please let Miss Price in. She is with the Sheriff's department and has some documents for us. Even better. We are at the yellow garage area. Thanks." I push the red button to end the call.

"The intern from Josh's office?" Olivia asks.

"Yes. The guy at the gate is having someone bring her over in a golf cart."

"Everything fine?" I hadn't noticed that Hans and Margarite stealthily had moved behind me.

"Yes. Thank you for asking. Just some papers are being delivered", I reply.

"Thomas, we heard about the two couriers who were transporting a significant quantity of drugs being killed near the Homestead race track. We were not sure that the murders are related to your most welcome presence, but maybe so. You may not be aware, but certain people believe that there is a likely connection between the racing and the drugs."

Margarite does not waste words. I cannot fathom how these folks are always *spot on.*

I am saved by the bell as Eleanor Price arrives in an official Daytona golf cart. She literally jumps out and runs over to us with the envelope. The contents may not be as exciting as the Academy Awards, but I am looking forward to reading the documents. "Ms. Price, I would like you to meet Madam and Monsieur Leiter. Eleanor brought with her what I hope will be enlightening information."

Always the hostess, Margarite asks, "Miss Price, have you eaten?"

"Oh, thank you but I am expected home shortly."

"Eleanor and her father will be our guests on Saturday and Sunday."

"Then you shall definitely be expected to join us for post race festivities," Margarite speaks in a way that a simple statement is really a command and no one questions it.

"Thanks." The young intern waves as she jumps back into the cart.

"Hopefully she just brought us some useful fingerprint and financial information, which seems to relate to same issue which you mentioned and about which we need to discuss in further detail."

"Agreed." Hans says. "Tomorrow morning you will be here for a ride with Cecil. Let us all meet in our house on wheels for a light breakfast after. *N'est pas?*"

"Oui."

"Trés bon. Let us return to the activities. I am to understand that a fabulous dessert has been prepared and several of the other drivers have told me that they want to entertain us with, how you say, down home country music. I am very much looking forward to their performance." Margarite and Hans begin to walk back to the feast-hand in hand.

"I am speechless," I say to Olivia.

"Do you think we should get Josh's approval before we share everything?"

"Detective Nederfield, may I remind you that the mean old crab is recovering from having undergone a battery of medical testing and should not be disturbed. And second, do you think he would object to getting help from the Bentley Seven?"

"And Hudson one." Olivia starts to laugh. "Since I do not believe in coincidences and I am not sure that divine intervention should be considered as a factor, let's go with the flow. These folks have at least a combined 250 years of experience doing things we cannot imagine. It is spooky, but there is no one I want to be working a murder case with than Hans, Margarite, Pierre, Stanford, Franco, Charles and Frederick, and if Cecil is Charles' brother, he can be added to the list."

"I absolutely agree. Let us partake of an after dinner sweet, a little music and maybe liquid refreshment."

"Don't forget that we have a lot of documents to read tonight." Detective Nederfield can be such a party pooper sometimes. Since we are trying to follow the money, maybe the information Eleanor brought us about Treasury bonds, bills and notes from Montgomery's safe deposit box will help. What about the fingerprints? We do have a lot of work ahead of us, but the sound of a fiddle, banjo and several guitars draws us like a magnet to the source of the music and the dessert and the tubs of beers from every known brewery in the world-or so it seems.

"One of the things I like most about car racing is the feeling of camaraderie. Not at the professional level but at the lower end and certainly among the vintage folks," Olivia observes as the drivers, crew members and miscellaneous others pull up chairs from the dinner table and circle the band, plates on their laps and beer in their hands.

Margarite once again takes control. For such a small woman with a relatively small voice, she can be heard for miles. Why? Because everyone is as quiet a mouse when she rises to speak. "Gathered friends, I want to extend a special thanks to Stanford and Franco whom you all know and their crew of young men and women for a fantastic dinner. How much the rest of the world misses by not eating smoked brisket with all the fixin's. In keeping with thc true tradition of stock car racing, about which I am learning a great deal, several of our extended family members have agreed to play for us. I have been assured that their musical career and racing career transcend decades and with no further ado I would like to introduce Felix Cassidy on banjo and mandolin, Bubba Whitestone on guitar, Tyler Stephens on bass guitar and Marlene Robbins vocalist and fiddler extraordinaire. In real life Felix drives the white number 31 Ford, Bubba wrestles a red Chrysler around, Tyler's energy is focused on the number 12 black Oldsmobile and Marlene guides a turquoise and white Chevrolet. Let's give them a round of applause." Margarite is beaming from ear to ear. She is in her element. I'll bet in another life she was a stage actress. Maybe earlier in this life.

"I am exhausted," Olivia whispers. Since it is now after ten o'clock, and we have been here eating, drinking and listening to the best country music I have heard outside of

Nashville. I get it. Fortunately, everyone present will be competing tomorrow and so we all bid *good evening* to one and all and trek back to the Airstream.

CHAPTER TWENTY-FIVE

It's not the alarm that wakes me; it's the smell of freshly brewed hazelnut coffee that lifts the fog from my eyes, served by the most beautiful Oliver Nederfield, wrapped in a British racing green terry cloth bath robe. After a couple of sips, I struggle to my feet, am handed a large towel and my Dopp kit and told to get myself to the showers, which are actually near by, clean and have hot water. A usually rare occurrence at a race track, but this is Daytona.

"We never went over the documents," I moan.

"What means *we* Special Detective Ballard? Good thing I can tell you everything in about one minute. Every financial instrument in Montgomery's safe deposit box was purchased by one Cosmo Costello as trustee of the Tessa Family Trust at the Providence branch of the Island Trust Company which has another branch in the Grand Cayman. My guess, Uncle Cosmo gave each instrument to his nephew with instructions to put them in the box. Fingerprints inconclusive."

"How much are we talking about?" I ask.

"Roughly four million dollars."

"That's a lot of lettuce." I reply.

"I think we need to get the records of the Tessa Family Trust. My instincts are screaming at me *to follow the money.*"

"Agreed, but how?"

"Not sure yet, but you have got to get a move on it. Off to the showers. I'll refill your coffee if you are a good boy and wash behind your ears. Out!"

I have to admit that a hot shower and an even hotter cup of coffee make me feel like I am ready for anything, except finding a killer or killers, a lot of drugs before they get to the street and blowing the lid off of an increasingly deadly cycle of murder, money and cocaine. No problem.

Olivia and I briskly walk over to the yellow garages. I don't want to miss a ride on the iconic oval at Daytona Speedway in an equally iconic Hudson Hornet. I feel a story simmering in the back of my mind. Last night's feast has made way for the chaos that always precedes a race. Everyone is moving around in sort of a weird dance-checking oil, tire pressure, safety equipment and making sure that every little bug has been removed from the windshield. Since this is purely an exhibition event, staged largely for sponsors, there are a lot of people simply milling around waiting for instructions-Olivia and I included.

Because of a noise ordinance dating from the middle-ages, race car engines cannot be started until 7:30 on week-days and 8:00 on weekends and holidays. The only residential area near the track is at least two miles away and is a newly built high end type resort. Suddenly the air is filled with sounds that can only be generated by old school V-8 engines. Music to my ears. We are hustled over to the Hudson by Frederick and Charles. Most of the vintage stock cars are still fitted with so-called bench seats, so stuffing into the front is no problem. We each have a lap belt. I guess we will be cruising at a fairly modest speed.

Conversation is impossible. Cecil gives us a *thumbs-up* as the fire breathing motor monsters of yore move out onto the track. The Hudson is unique in that it was designed to step down into rather than step up into. It feels like you are only inches off the pavement, which you are. Even at this early hour the stands are filling up with spectators who want to get their money's worth. We wave-they wave and everyone has a great time, except that our tour is way too short.

"How did you enjoy your jaunt in the jalopy?" Cecil asks as we return to the garage area.

"I can't believe you drive these cars at over 100 miles per hour." Olivia says. "What a thrill."

"For higher speeds, we remove the bench seat and install a current style race seat with plenty of side support and of course we have a six point harness system. That pretty much eliminates the slide around inside the car problem."

"When do you get back on the track?" I ask.

"Not until around one. This session serves two purposes: it makes sure the cars and the drivers are awake and moving without parts falling off and is great promotion for the sport and its rich history. I understand that we have a breakfast appointment." Cecil starts to walk toward a huge motor home and enclosed trailer combination.

"I guess everyone knows," Olivia observes

"Only those that Hans and Margarite believe need to know," I reply.

"The Bentley Seven."

"And Hudson one." We hold hands and skip walk toward breakfast. Safely stowed in Detective Nederfield's pocket book is everything we have gathered so far in our side of the investigation.

The hustle and bustle has slowed to a less frenetic pace, but nevertheless each car is getting the TLC deserved by these wondrous machines-and those who drive and maintain them.

"Bon jour," Margarite responds to my knock on the door of their incredible house on wheels, painted none other than British racing green with subtle yellow pin stripes along its 45 foot expanse.

"Bon jour," Olivia and I respond together.

"Before we talk, we must eat. Come." Margarite leads us into the dining area, which with the two sliders fully extended is about 18' x 18' and certainly big enough for breakfast for ten. After being handed a cup of heavenly smelling coffee by the ubiquitous Franco and saying "good morning" to everyone, we are seated next to Margarite and Hans.

"Pardon the meager offerings," Stanford begins, "But a working breakfast was not planned and I have had to make do."

His definition of making do includes several different types of freshly baked pastries, an egg and cheese casserole, which melts in your mouth, fresh fruit compote, assorted homemade jellies and jams and sausage links, which we are told are made from turkey.

CHAPTER TWENTY-SIX

After breakfast is cleared, Pierre asks us all to step outside for a moment so that he can rearrange the RV's interior for our meeting. How much rearranging can one do to an RV? The sky is bright blue; temperature is in the low 70s, standing next to Olivia sipping a demitasse of something which smells delicious, how much better can it get?

We are forthwith summonsed into our dining room now converted into a high tech conference room with not one, but two 55-inch monitors mounted on the wall. As expected Hans is the first to speak.

"I must admit that automotive events are getting far more interesting since Olivia and Thomas have entered our world. While we all hoped that you would be attending the race, I, for one, never imagined that circumstances would find us looking into what might be related crimes. Briefly said, we were asked several months ago to inquire of our resources whether or not illegal drug activity has increased in the automotive venues we attend. The source of the request is multi-jurisdictional which may explain why we were approached." Hans draws a long sip from his coffee cup. I, for one, don't want to know who, nor should I say what organizations sought out help from the Bentley Seven-plus one. I do know that they are the best.

"May I ask a question?" Olivia raises her hand bringing back memories of third grade.

"By all means," Margarite replies.

"Since our investigation is only about a week old, do you think it might be easier if we tell you what we know, which isn't a lot; what we surmise, which is somewhat more; and what we can only guess at, which is most everything."

"As always, the beautiful Detective Nederfield has cut to the chase," our chef, now active member of the investigative team, Stanford, adds.

"May I?" I look at Olivia, who nods. "We put this matrix together last night. We have not connected very many dots but I predict that your work will overlay some of ours." I hand each of the eight members a piece of paper on which we have photographs and brief biographies of Cosmo and his nephew. I have also added Henry Fuller with a dotted line to both Don Montgomery and Juan Carlos for no other reason than gut instinct. I don't feel solid about the about the way data kind of peters out. I wonder if the Bentley gang can help us get the records involving the Tessa Family Trust.

"Thomas, this is actually more helpful than the expression on your face suggests. Cosmo Costello's name has come up in several discussions, but mostly as a mid level broker. He seems to introduce buyers and sellers of mostly cocaine and more recently opioids to one another and takes a commission based on the value of the drugs. Why is he on your chart?"

"He was murdered last weekend. He was killed after answering the door to his house and his body dumped at the county landfill. The weapon of choice was a large caliber handgun at close range. We were told that the timing coincided with a missing shipment of cocaine which disappeared on route to Homestead-Miami Speedway which was the venue at which Cosmo's nephew, Donald Montgomery, was participating. Also the couriers were later found dead from multiple knife wounds. The deceased funded Montgomery's race program, and his own life style, which was very modest, by funds from a Rhode Island family trust, whose records we have not yet seen. There does not seem to be anything that connects Montgomery to drugs other than the business activities of his uncle, about which he didn't know or care to know. We were going to pursue the missing cocaine connection, but our boss told us the DEA was on it and they were likely to have it covered, especially since they lost it."

"And how is Sheriff McCarthy?" Margarite asks.

"Basically overworked and overweight. We hope he will be here on Saturday. May we tell him of your presence here and the discussions we are having?"" Olivia is very careful in choosing her words.

"I would like to defer answering that question until our briefing is done. Our contacts appear to be unaware of Mr. Costello's death, the manner of his death and the connection with a race car driver. Our missions definitely overlap and I can say that we all are pleased to be once again reunited, albeit in rather unsavory circumstances."

"Unsavory, my dear brother-in-law? I think that you are insulting both Franco and Stanford, who have served us wonderful food. Unsavory indeed." Pierre laughs at his own play on words. Insulting fine cuisine is done in front of a Frenchman at one's peril.

"Touché, *mon frerè*"

Despite the seriousness of the task, these folks are still able to retain a sense of humor and of perspective-special qualities in this day and age.

Margarite starts to clap her hands to get everyone's attention. "We must use our time wisely."

I glance at my watch and note that we have a little more than an hour before our meeting with Don Montgomery.

"Thomas, do you have a time issue?" Charles, the keen eyed photographer asks.

"Actually, we have a meeting with young Montgomery at 11:00," I reply. "He doesn't know about Costello's death. Now that the landscape has expanded, maybe we should postpone until we know more."

"I think that the meeting should go forward but I propose that Charles attend. We can introduce him as a photo journalist. His credentials are impeccable and he knows everything we know." Hans, as usual, articulates the logical course of action.

"I will bring some examples of my work and a camera or two, so when the young man arrives he will not be off put. Is he to be trusted or shall we keep him at arm's length?"

"May I suggest that we make on the spot decisions," Olivia suggests.

"Très bon. Let us proceed as best we can with the briefing." Margarite once again is at the helm.

Suddenly both computer monitors come to life.

CHAPTER TWENTY-SEVEN

That was the fastest hour and a half briefing I have ever attended, although I admit to having limited experience. I rise and say, "Olivia and I have to meet Mr. Montgomery in fifteen minutes and I need to stretch my legs, so we will walk. Charles, do you want to join us?"

"Thank you Thomas, but I have to pull a few things together and then ask Franco to give me a lift over to your trailer if that is alright with you."

"Perfect."

"I'll bring a Thermos of coffee and some snacks when I deliver Charles," Franco volunteers.

This army never fights on an empty stomach. Olivia and I leave the *Ritz on wheels* and head to our humble abode. "What did you think?" I ask.

"This is like super big time. I bet half of the law enforcement community is involved."

"As members of a county sheriff's office we are way down the food chain."

"Except, my dear Thomas, our dear friends are certainly very close to the top, so that I am sure we will get every consideration."

"I hope we will be able to add something to the investigation," I suggest.

"If Don Montgomery is an all-America kid, as I suspect, he may be a key. The distribution logistics of moving so much cocaine must be incredibly complicated." Olivia is obviously considering our relatively minor problem: solve a murder.

"When I interviewed Cosmo about organized crime and car racing, he really did not consider the gambling aspect anything significant and certainly not large enough to warrant *his kind* to get involved. Maybe that's why he was supportive of his nephew's participation. The sport was dangerous, but not dirty . . . until now." I think I should re-read my article.

"You have to admit that the plan is brilliant: move a lot of drugs to a lot of places throughout the country with little risk of detection. Why? Because stock car racing is as wholesome as apple pie." Olivia is spot on. Maybe there is a connection between Cosmo Costello's death and drugs, but not in the way we initially imagined.

"Chez Ballard, my dear," I quip. Opening the door to my-our classic Airstream. We were quick out the door this morning so a little tidying up is in order and just in time. Franco's golf cart comes to a screeching halt at our door and Charles alights looking like he is ready for a safari; cameras slung over his shoulder, jacket with pockets bulging with photographic stuff and a leather flat brief case.

"I will bring in your coffee and some special treats Stanford put together," Franco announces. He uncovers a tray resting on the back seat with a flourish. *"Eccola. Magnificent, sì?"*

"Franco, it is so much," Olivia says. "But it is indeed magnificent." Pastries, melon wrapped with prosciutto, jams and fresh butter.

Charles busies himself with putting his gear on our all purpose table which is miniscule in comparison to the one in the Bentley Seven RV. He opens his leather case and removes dozens of black and white photographs of many of the cars competing this weekend, including Don Montgomery's, which I pick up and say, "Nice touch, Charles."

"I slipped out of the briefing and took a few shots of the young man's car. I have a small darkroom in the back of the trailer. I thought it would explain my presence here."

Olivia looks at me with one of her *did you expect anything different* looks.

"Call me . . . whenever," Franco says as he leaves the trailer.

"Ciao," Olivia replies.

"Hans was very particular about not wanting to give the young driver a lot of information. He trusts your judgment about the chap's character and is sure that you will be able to ascertain how much he knows about the scope of our investigation. If you both approve his credibility, Hans wants to set up another team meeting with everyone present. Information will be provided on a need to know basis initially. Caution is today's password." Charles chuckles.

"We both agree. The scope of this is far, far beyond the murder of Montgomery's uncle," I add.

"Or maybe not," Olivia posits. "I can envision a scenario where Costello's death has everything to do with the big picture and very little to do with the small picture which we are exploring."

"Spill the beans most brilliant and lovely one," I quip.

Depending on your point of view, the knock on the trailer's door is opportune.

"Enter!" I shout.

"Am I disturbing you?" Montgomery stammers as he enters.

"Au contraire," Charles answers.

"Don, I would like you to meet Charles who has been a photo journalist forever, specializing in just about everything, but today . . . automobiles."

"And the people who drive them and watch them being driven. For example, the pizza delivery man." Charles hands Don a picture of his number 16 Ford with a large pizza slice logo on the side which says *Tessa Pizza-old country taste.*

"Wow! This is great. When did you take it?"

"This morning. During your warm up. I find it easier to get individual images during early practice sessions."

"It is fantastic. Wait! Are you Charles Llewellyn? I saw an exhibit you did at the Museum of Modern Art last year. My uncle took me there. It was outrageous. The car photos were cool, but the way you captured horses and their jockeys was so terrific. There was one I remember. The horse's name was Marvelous Monet and it looked like it was running at the front. The expression on both the horse and rider was so serene. Not what I expected. I am truly honored."

"Olivia, my dear, please bring me a glass of water before I swoon." Charles is obviously teasing. "The MOMA exhibit was great fun. Where ever I show, I pick a theme. That time I selected competitive speed. And as a gift to one so young with such good taste in photography, I will print a copy of the image for you."

"Really? Wait 'til I tell Uncle Cosmo."

"Don . . . please sit down. There is no easy way to say this, but your uncle is dead. He was murdered over the weekend. How much do you know about what your uncle did for a living?"

One could hear a pin drop. Tears formed in the corner of the young man's eyes.

"I was hoping that he could distance himself from all that. He told the big shots in Providence that he was going to retire. He wanted to spend more time with me. My parents died about three years ago and Uncle Cosmo is all I have. And I was all he had. Family is important to people like my uncle and the people up North understood and gave him their blessing. They were planning on having the Tessa Pizza chain, which was named after my mother, be my sponsor so I could have the best race car equipment. They thought that an Italian in stock car racing was a good image. And they owed Uncle Cosmo." Olivia hands him a tissue.

"Don, you said they thought an Italian in stock car racing was good for the image."

"Oh, you mean Montgomery? My birth father was Giovanni Pasatti. He was killed when I was about four. I really don't remember him except he seemed so big and full of energy. He died in the line of duty. He was a cop in Providence. Because he was Sicilian, he and the big shots were able to keep a lid on drugs and gang violence. Unfortunately, he was in the wrong place at the wrong time and was killed during a domestic dispute. My uncle stepped in and took care of us. We all moved to Orlando and Uncle Cosmo was set up to run about a dozen pizza parlors. I suspect he did other things, but no one ever spoke of it. My mother met my step father a couple of years later. He was a musician and played in lots of clubs. Again, it was a family thing, but I was too young to know or care. William Montgomery and my mom got married when I was eight. I remember a big Italian wedding. Literally it was a scene from *Godfather.* Old ladies pinching my cheeks and big men with cigars slapping me on the back and saying how much I'd grown. I never knew these people had ever seen me when I was small. May I have some water?"

I quickly retrieve a chilled bottle from the fridge. I am quite sure this kid is absolutely being straight. I am still a little fuzzy about the connection to Costello's murder.

"Uncle Cosmo bought us a house, next door to his of course and for the next ten years I had the basic Central Florida upbringing. I loved cars and sometimes we would have a family outing at the races. When I was accepted at University of Central Florida, I wanted to stay at home but my mom, step dad and uncle all convinced me that I needed to embrace the college experience. During my freshman year I decided I wanted to be an engineer and really worked hard. I got straight A's and Uncle Cosmo bought me a late model sportsman. My parents weren't thrilled, but he convinced them that I was a smart and considerate kid and that racing was a great place to apply theoretical engineering knowledge. How he ever came up with that line, I never knew, but it worked. My step dad got a gig on a TV show and my parents headed out to California for what was to be a month or so. They never returned. They were both killed in a huge accident in L.A. I stayed at UCF and continued to work hard because that is what they would have wanted. All my school bills were paid by a trust and a got an allowance as well. Not a lot, but enough that I never had to do stupid things to get money. I continued to race whenever I could. Uncle Cosmo agreed to have the pizza shops sponsor me but only up to a certain amount. He made me do a budget each season and that was all I got. I learned to take care of my car mechanically both on and off the track. I never pushed beyond what the car was capable of. I thought reliability and consistency were the attributes which would allow me to compete at any level."

"Can you think of any reason your uncle was murdered?"

"That's a really hard question to answer Mr. Ballard. I grew up with the understanding that we were protected from those kinds of things. I remember in high school, there were a couple of kids picking on a younger student. I told them to leave him alone. They started to mouth off and I figured I was going to have to fight. Suddenly everything grew quiet. I looked around and saw a huge man get out of a black Lincoln and start to walk toward me. He pointed at the group of older kids and pointed like up the street. Nothing was said, but those boys took off running. The big guy touched the rim of his hat, turned and got back in the car. Nobody would touch my uncle who valued their life. Nobody. His retirement did not create a vacuum. Everyone was on board. I do remember that Uncle Cosmo got into s very loud altercation with some people I didn't recognize at the Speedway at Fruitfield near Palm Beach about three weeks ago. I couldn't hear them but Uncle Cosmo kept pointing at my trailer and then at them. I was concerned at first but my uncle could take care of himself and always carried a weapon or two, although I never saw him fire a gun in anger. He frequently took me to the pistol range and we practiced for hours. I am proficient, but he was absolutely unbelievable. A guy who was an FBI agent would always search out my uncle whenever he got a new weapon and ask for tips about the gun. Anyway, the discussion ended and the two guys walked away. Uncle Cosmo didn't move a muscle for at least ten minutes."

"Young man, can you identify the other men?" Charles asks.

"I think so."

"Good. Let's start with the shape of the face." Charles had pulled a sketch pad and pencil from his case. For the next ten minutes he talked Don through the identification process. "How's this?" Charles turns the pad toward the young man.

"Unbelievable. It was like you took a photograph."

"I simply translated your observations onto paper."

"Don't ask," Olivia whispers.

"Don, when are next scheduled to drive?" I ask. Both Olivia and Charles nod.

"I have qualifying at 2:00, but I am really bummed out about Uncle Cosmo."

"He would have wanted you to race and race your best," Charles inserts.

"Can you meet us in the yellow garages at 6:00?" I inquire.

"Quite simply young man, we are not exactly what we seem. Ms Nederfield is a detective with the Orange County Sheriff's department and Mr. Ballard is a deputy, as well as a wonderful writer. My photography has taken me across each continent observing and recording people, places and events. I am telling you this because I want you to meet the rest of our team. We are investigating your uncle's death in conjunction with a very large and serious problem. I can assure you that the cause and the perpetrators will not remain a mystery. You have been candid with us and I want to be candid with you. Our group is very experienced and very competent and you may be of use to us in reviewing the information we are gathering . . . connecting the dots." That is certainly the largest number of words I have heard Charles utter. He has made an executive decision, but obviously still wants feedback from the others.

"Connecting the dots?"

"It is an expression we use to describe the process of solving crimes. We try to connect pieces of evidence with people in an effort to answer the basic who, what, where, why, and how." Olivia's voice is calming.

"You have worked together before?"

"That we have," Charles answers as he returns his pictures into the leather file. "I'm calling Franco for a ride. I will discuss matters with Hans and Margarite. Mr. Montgomery, after our meeting at 6:00, we are planning a special dinner. Please join us." As pleasant as Charles tries to make it sound, his invitation was a bit more of an order than a request.

"How will I know where to find you?"

"When you arrive at the yellow garages, just ask."

"For whom?"

Obviously Don Montgomery is totally confused. "The Bentley Seven!" We three answer together and start to laugh.

CHAPTER TWENTY-EIGHT

After both the young driver and the old photographer leave, I feel relieved, largely because I had dreaded telling Montgomery about his uncle's death. They were obviously close and the impact has not even scratched the surface-but it will.

"I like to think that I am a pretty good judge of character and Donald Montgomery is the real deal. I cannot imagine he is involved in any way in his Cosmo's death or the drugs," Olivia comments.

"I agree and he may be of help, although I think that Hans is on *a need to know* basis with even us."

"Thomas, you are a cynic, although I tend to think that there may be even more to this investigation than the Bentley Seven has told us. In their defense we only had about ninety minutes to be briefed on something I think has been kicking around for months."

"We've got to meet Juan Carlos at noon and Cecil is practicing at 12:30. I also want to see what magic the Bentley Seven conjure up regarding the image Charles drew."

"We've got about thirty minutes. I think we should call Josh and bring him up to speed." Olivia doesn't want to make the boss unhappy.

"Good idea." I speed dial his private number which, of course, is answered by Helen. "Good morning Helen, is the Sheriff up and about?"

"Glad you called, Thomas. Sheriff McCarthy has been a real crab all day. The doctor wants him to reduce his caffeine intake by a zillion per cent. Two cups of coffee and one Dr. Pepper per day. He is climbing the walls."

"Please inform the exalted one that we need to talk to him. He is still on pay roll, right?"

"You are so cruel, but absolutely correct. I'll round him up and have him call you right back."

"Please. We have a small window and a lot to go over."

"I have a spooky feeling," Olivia announces. "When we had our briefing this morning, it was only the Bentley Seven, Cecil and the two of us."

"Yeh, that's right. So?"

"The so is that this investigation has international as well as domestic ramifications. It has a very major drug component, as well as a couple of murders . . . that we know about. And yet there was not a single representative of any law enforcement community."

"And?"

"Either the Bentley Seven are flying solo, or they are the entire law enforcement community."

Olivia is right except that our briefing was short, but comprehensive, and pretty damn case specific. "I'm voting for the latter."

"I agree. We really don't know much about the Bentley Seven except that they are brilliant, efficient, experienced and well trained." Olivia states the obvious.

"And extremely well connected."

Saved by the bell or at least the buzzing sound of my cell. "It's Josh." I answer. "Good morning. I am putting you on speaker so Olivia can participate in what will be short and sweet. Cosmo's death is the tip of an iceberg, but does not seem to have turf war implications."

"How did you get to that conclusion?" Sheriff McCarthy's voice booms.

"Boss, the Bentley Seven is here with an addition to the group, Charles' brother Cecil, who is a computer whizz kid, albeit a senior. They briefed us early this morning. I have a sense that they are representing the interests of a lot of folks, including Interpol, D.E.A., probably F.B.I. and most likely everyone else. Subtle, but that's their style. Cecil is racing a vintage stock car which seems to be their cover. We met with Don Montgomery. Told him about Uncle Cosmo. We think he is a straight shooter. We've got an interview with another young driver in a few minutes." Olivia relinquishes the phone to me.

"Josh, my gut reaction is that we are talking about nationwide maybe worldwide distribution ramifications, not someone trying to encroach on Costello, who, according to his nephew, was retiring with the blessing of Providence."

"How can I help?" Sheriff McCarthy asks.

"Not sure. We are meeting with Hans and the rest of the team to watch Cecil practice at 12:30 and then we will probably go into executive session. I'll ask him then."

"Olivia and you too Thomas, be careful. I have to say there is no one I would rather be covering my backside than the Bentley gang. How do they do it? I'm 44 and have to watch what I eat and drink, get more exercise and lose a lot of weight. They are all over 70 and fit as fiddles. It's not fair."

"Quit whining and stop feeling sorry for yourself. Helen has reported that you are being a pill around the office." Olivia has only been with the Sheriff's office for a few years, yet she is probably as respected as any officer on the force. And outspoken.

"Josh, we will call you by three. Plan on coming out here tomorrow unless otherwise advised." I am not being disrespectful to the Sheriff of Orange County, just being his best friend for almost 40 of those 44 years.

"Talk with you both later." End of conversation.

"I'm going to freshen up and then we have to head over to the Driver's Lounge," Olivia announces. "I suggest you do the same . . . out there." She points to the concrete building housing the men's room. I know what the expression *being sent to the showers means.* I am not looking forward to meeting with Juan Carlos. I am not sure why.

CHAPTER TWENTY-NINE

The *Driver's Lounge* at a track like Daytona stands in marked contrast to the pop up tent with a charcoal grill at most tracks. It is a little like comparing the Ritz to McDonalds. Not only is it air conditioned with a view of the track, but it is furnished with designer furniture in designer colors and features a full service restaurant, except no liquor while the track is "hot", which means until all the racing for the day is over. There are small rooms in which drivers, sponsors and even journalists can chat about-whatever. Upon entering, all male heads snap around to look at Olivia. If I wasn't so secure in our relationship I would have a massive case of the jealousies. She loves it. A couple of times when we have entered into a room, she gets the whiplash look from the assembled men and then ever so slowly she pulls her badge from her pocket book and loops the chain over her neck. I then do the same. The reaction is priceless. We can't do that here because we are simply a couple of journalists interviewing a young driver, whom we spot in the corner with several young ladies wearing what I call stockcar nothing. You know the type, short shorts, blouses that are too tight and big hair. I have researched racing over the last 100 years and there always seems to have been a bevy of beauties wearing stockcar nothing. Oh well.

"Juan Carlos, *còmo estàs?"* I announce our presence.

"I didn't know you spoke Spanish," Olivia remarks.

"I grew up in Orlando, remember?"

The young driver waves and leaves his admirers, but not without giving each of them a kiss-on the cheek. "Hola," Juan Carlos shouts although he is only about three feet away. Must be all the noise from the engine that causes him to speak loudly.

"How was your practice?" I ask.

"Fantastic. If it had been an official qualifying, I would be gridded in the top ten. Señor Fuller is very pleased. I think he may offer me a ride for the weekend."

"I wish you the best of luck. In the few minutes we have, I want to get a lot of background information directly from you. I want to know things like *what got you interested in racing? Who are your backers, supporters and sponsors? What difference do you see in racing here and Argentina?"*

"Do you mind if we use one of the small rooms. I want to tape record you if that is okay." Olivia says, oozing with charm.

"Oh sure. That's great." We walk toward the closest available room. I don't want to be responsible for some driver being injured watching Olivia sashay across the lounge.

"Tell me about yourself," Detective Nederfield begins.

"I was born in Buenos Aires. My mother died when I was four and my father remarried shortly thereafter to a woman named Bo-hyun. At first we did not get along. I guess I missed my mother and she was trying to fit in. It turns out that her brother is Jai-hyun Kim."

"That name sounds familiar," Olivia comments.

"It should, he is the son of the founder of Kim Enterprises, one of the world's largest conglomerates. The Kim empire is huge and diverse, including performance tires. Any connections?" I ask.

"You are very astute Mr. Ballard. My father is a rancher but became the distributor of Kim tires in all of South America and now even North America. When I started to show an interest and some skill in racing, I was fully sponsored. My father did not really want me to race, thought it was a waste of time, but decided it would be best if I had the finest equipment available. Even Mr. Kim came to several races while he was traveling in Argentina and watched me compete. I was very lucky."

"Racing in South America and in North America differs in one significant way: Each type of racing has a lead tire sponsor. In stockcar racing Goodyear dominates at the top level and Hoosier at the lower levels. Indy cars use Firestone. Formula One mostly races on Michelin tires and vintage sports car racing is pretty much a Dunlop show. In South America, it's much more of an open playground and there is a lot of competition. Newcomers like Kim are vying for a large share of the performance market, mostly small cars and have a strategy that includes all levels of racing. Needless to say, there has been a lot of resistance here."

"You are very well informed Mr. Ballard."

"It's my job Juan Carlos, but I want to know about you."

"I won the stock sedan championship last year in Argentina, on Kim tires. It was decided I should come to the U.S. and race, but even with full sponsorship, getting a ride is difficult until you prove yourself to the others."

"It makes sense. Most drivers want to think that their competition is competent and safe." Olivia has a really good handle on racing and those that race.

"I know, but I was very . . . how do you say . . . hyper. Bo-hyun was very helpful in making me relax and see what she calls the *whole world.* I went to the smaller tracks and raced . . . always on Kim tires and always with a very good car."

"Money helps when you are racing."

"Some others resented it. They had been driving for years and were very good and I know that they would have beaten me if I had to drive their cars or they drove my car. But I did not let that bother me. It was not the way it was and I won and I am here and they are not."

Smug little punk, I say to myself.

"Did you come here to race all alone?" Olivia asks.

Interesting question. I am not sure where she is going with it.

"No. My father sent two mechanics with me. And Bo-hyun was worried about kidnapping or something so her youngest brother Jung is here also. He's a little scary but that is probably good. In Argentina, there are few people with guns."

Other than the military. I am talking to myself again.

"What does Henry Fuller think of your sponsorship?" The astute Detective Nederfield asks.

"We haven't talked about it much."

"Did you practice on Kim tires" I inquire.

"Not in his car, but I did have them on my car when I practiced earlier this morning. I want to try the new super speedway design. If I can put them on Mr. Fuller's car for a couple of laps, I can really get a good comparison."

There is no way the team is going to piss off Goodyear at Daytona. Maybe in a private practice session.

"Juan Carlos, do you think it is likely that a major team is going to jeopardize their relationship with Goodyear?"

"Maybe, if I am faster on Kim tires. Jung Kim is here and he can be very persuasive. He wants to set up dealerships for his high performance radials all over the United States. He has done well in California but it is harder in the South." Juan Carlos shrugs.

It is a gesture of indifference and arrogance. While I will admit he has performed well at the lower level of the circuit, as he points out, he has far better equipment. This is big time and big money is involved. Very big money, which leads me to Henry Fuller.

"We wish you the very best of luck. If you do get a ride with Team Fuller, and if you do convince him to let you try Kim tires on one of his cars, please invite me to the demonstration." Olivia and I both shake hands with Señor Cidado and leave.

"His hand feels like a dead fish," Olivia whispers.

CHAPTER THIRTY

As we make our exit, Olivia whispers to me, "Arrogant twerp".

Assuming she is referring to the young Argentinean driver, I say, "I agree. He is in a whole other game now and he is not going to be taking that attitude for long."

"He is not in the same league as the big boys and Juan Carlos is going to be roughed up a bit and his bodyguard won't be able to do much about it." Olivia's statement echoes my sentiments exactly.

"Let's head over to Bentley central. I want to watch the old timer's race around the oval. It will bring back memories of Smokey, Fireball, Le Roy, Junior, Tiny and Freddie."

"Not to mention some Lee, Buck and Speedy."

"Another era, when drivers started running bootleg at ten or eleven rather than driving go-karts."

"Thomas, nostalgia is getting the best of you."

"I'm also getting hungry."

"Now there's a surprise." Detective Nederfield can be so mean.

Walking through the garage area at Daytona is the auto journalist equivalent of a golfer walking the course at Augusta. Suddenly, Olivia grabs my arm.

"Thomas, look over there." She points in the direction of a huge semi-trailer with the name Goodyear on its side, flanked by stacks of tires and several machines for mounting and balancing. Two men are arguing; a smallish man wearing a business suit with his back toward us and a giant of a man wear white coveralls with the Goodyear logo on the front. Whatever they are saying is very animated. The smaller man keeps pointing to an ATV with a trailer filled with tires. Every once in a while the smaller man would point his finger at the Goodyear man. It's comical because instead of the old *finger in the chest* it was more like the *finger in the belt buckle.* Although we can't hear it ring, the smaller man's cell obviously is summonsing him. He looks at the screen, shakes his head, turns and marches off toward the ATV.

Olivia releases my arm and reaches into her giant carry everything purse. Everything includes a very scary looking Glock 9mm.

If I had a giant purse I would be doing the same thing. The smaller man is the spitting image of the character Charles drew from Don Montgomery's description of man with whom his uncle had been arguing two weeks ago.

"This is creepy," I whisper.

The ATV rattles off toward the blue garage area where the competitors from the support races park their rigs.

"Let's get back and see if Hans has been able to identify the person in Charles' drawing."

"I agree. The features of this guy are definitely Asian and he has a load of tires."

"Kim?"

"Too much of a coincidence and . . ."

"We don't believe in coincidences." Olivia and I answer together.

The yellow garage area is a bee hive of activity in advance of the first practice for the vintage class. Frederick passes us with a clip board in hand and shouts as he hustles by, "Please don't think me rude. I want to change the spark plugs on the Hudson before Cecil goes on the track."

"Understood," I reply. I didn't think any further answered was warranted.

"Lunch will be served after the practice session," Stanford says as he and Franco quick time toward the pits.

"A lot of action at Team Bentley," Olivia observes. "Do you think Hans and Margarite are in the trailer?"

"No, we are off to the pits," the couple answers in tandem as they approach us from behind the Hudson's trailer. Hans is clutching his tablet and two hand-held speed guns for timing. Margarite has a stop watch on a silver chain, around her neck. "Thomas we have downloaded Charles' rendering and have been promised identification by the time we get back. He is with his brother getting him strapped into the car. Pierre is helping Marlene, the woman who was singing last night. Her mechanic showed up sick this morning."

"Posh. He was hung over and she was not going to let him touch that beautiful Chevrolet of hers. And my brother is always eager to help out a damsel in distress."

"The Gallant Gaul," I quip.

"Absolument. I trained him well. Let us go." Margarite marches us toward the pit.

It suddenly occurs to me that Team Bentley has traded their British racing green shirts for purple polo type shirts with the image of a hornet in white embroidered in the front pocket. The devil is in the detail.

"I want one of those shirts," Olivia whispers.

Before I can reply, we hear, "Mio Dio. Scusi. I ran so fast to keep up with Stanford; I forgot to give you these." Franco hands a purple shirt to Olivia and one to me and dashes off.

"Quickly, go to the RV and change. We will continue to walk to the pits, but slowly." Margarite has spoken. We scurry off.

"I love these folks," Olivia says as we exit the Bentley hotel on wheels.

"They miss nothing, nothing at all. Let's hurry so we can catch up to Margarite and Hans."

Suddenly Thor unleashes the thunder of thousands of horses as the vintage stock cars begin their journey to the pits. Cecil's pit crew has all assembled. My initial thought that this was going to be slow lap exhibition is dispelled quickly. Frederick arrives towing a small work shop behind the Bentley golf cart. He and Charles are wearing a fireproof pit suits and helmets. They quickly unload two five gallon gas cans, four tires and a jack. Franco is holding a purple sign with a white hornet at the end of a long pole. Stanford has a large black board with the letters POS on one side and LAP on the other. Margarite and Hans are seated in the elevated crew box behind the wall. We join them.

The cars slowly pull in front of their respective pits, stop, turn off their engines and somehow get out of their cars.

"Ladies and gentlemen," the track PA wails. "Please turn your attention to the main stage about half way down the front straightaway. The world famous University of Eastern Florida drum and bagel corps will accompany Florida's own Grammy nominated singer/song writer Ellie Griffin in the singing of our national anthem. Please rise and remove all hats."

When I was a kid, that last sentence would not have been necessary.

The stands are actually quite packed with spectators. As expected the infield is chock a block full with every assortment of vehicle imaginable. Many have been here for better than a week and will most likely stay another week, unless they run out of beer, which is highly unlikely. These are seriously experienced race car fans.

Each driver is introduced to the crowd. The announcer reads a little background about each of these stock car steeds, many of which have serious pedigrees, including Cecil's Hudson. Everyone is having a great time. In keeping with the pageantry of the occasion the mayor of Daytona Beach is today's grand marshal and screams into the microphone *"Driver's . . . start your engines!"*

Margarite taps my shoulder and hands me a pair of ear protectors, which she and Hans have already donned. She hands another pair to Olivia. The incredible sound from these engines is only somewhat reduced, but the likelihood of serious ear damage or migraine headache is lessened. Conversation is impossible except through the telecom system incorporated in the headphones. Hans is clearly the crew chief although Frederick is the wrench man and Charles is the gas man. I wonder how many laps in this session and how are they going to be gridded. The answer to the latter becomes self evident as the cars are released at five second intervals from their pits.

"They will run eight laps at speed and then come in. Each car has a transponder so that times can be instantly calculated and the grid is then established. The gridding is opposite for the afternoon session." Hans points to the button on the side of my headset, which I push.

"What do you mean by opposite?" I can see everyone on our team laugh at my question.

"This morning, the cars are gridded traditionally with the fastest car on the pole. This afternoon, the slowest car will be on the pole. It makes for fun racing, which is what it is all about."

"What a fantastic concept." I give a *thumbs up.*

CHAPTER THIRTY-ONE

"What a hoot," I exclaim removing my headphones after the completion of the first segment of this morning's session. After about four laps, the cob webs fall by trackside and these fire breathing monsters start to roll. The lines through the corners are all over the place which I attribute to the vastly different handling characteristics of each model. This was racing before the introduction of various aerodynamic packages which make the current stock car circuit, in my humble opinion, somewhat boring. Not only do the cars look the same, the cars are closely scrutinized to make sure each vehicle complies with this week's latest and greatest rules and regulations. The beasts on the track that we have been watching are easily identifiable. To watch the Fords up near the wall, the Chevrolets in the middle of the track and the step down Hudson just barely inside the lower edge of the track is exciting as well as nostalgic. Pack racing is not a term these guys use. If you can pass safely, do so, where ever and when ever. The lap times are faster now than when the cars raced in the 50s and early 60s because the cars use modern tires, although of the same size as originally raced. When all is said and done, most of these cars are lapping at speeds in excess of 100 miles per hours with top speeds around 125. Just the thought is scary, but these drivers really know their cars. There were no on track incidents, which for me is great. The fans who watch vintage racing of any kind have a better appreciation of preservation and performance than those who are always waiting for the *big one.* Also there is virtually no sponsorship money in vintage racing, so if you break it, you pay for it.

"Should we call Sheriff McCarthy?" Olivia asks.

"The race is only ten laps and then we can meet and bring one another up to speed. Then call the boss." I am not sure what we have learned except that Kim tires has a very aggressive sales and marketing program.

"I do not have a good feeling about this investigation," Detective Nederfield responds.

"Neither do I. Neither do I."

The race is as advertised, totally awesome. Missing was the pushing and shoving which marked period racing, except that a really rare Mercury banged into the wall on the back straight, causing a lot of paint removal but no structural damage. With the format for the next race, the Mercury looks like it will be on the pole. Team Hudson gathers its tools and heads back to race central. Other than Margarite, Hans, Olivia and I, the rest of the team, wearing their matching terry cloth Bentley bathrobes, head off to the showers to *freshen up.* Cecil's bathrobe is understandable purple. I stifle a laugh.

"They are a sight, aren't they?" Margarite comments.

Olivia and I chuckle, then without advanced warning, Detective Nederfield whistles loud enough to be heard five miles away and shouts, "Nice legs!"

The men respond with a wave.

Hans is laughing so hard, I am worried about him having a stroke. Margarite looks at me. I shrug. She cannot prevent herself from joining Hans in laughter.

"Is that a ladylike thing to do?" I ask with proverbial tongue in cheek.

"I was just practicing my police whistle. Just in case." To which I can think of no answer.

As some semblance of order returns, along with six scrubbed men, Hans gives me a photograph to look at. "Unbelievable!" The image is almost identical to Charles' rendering.

"Do you have an ID?" Olivia asks.

"He is Jung Kim, brother of Jai-hyun Kim present chief operating officer of Kim Enterprises," Hans replies.

"And sister of Bo-hyun Kim, step mother of Juan Carlos Cidado," I add.

"You have had a good morning. That piece of information was not sent to me." Hans seems pleased with me but upset with his source.

"Jung was sent here by his sister as a sort of body guard for young Juan Carlos He is obviously the man Don Montgomery saw arguing with his uncle a couple of weekends ago at Fruitfield Speedway."

"On the way over we saw him having what appeared to be a heated moment with the Goodyear man. We weren't close enough to hear anything they were saying," Olivia adds.

"Jung was also sent over by his brother to develop distributorships for Kim tires on the East coast. Car racing was one venue they wanted to use to promote their products."

Makes sense, except, why would Cosmo and Jung be talking about a tire dealership? Maybe he was trying to convince Cosmo to have young Montgomery race on Kim tires.

Hardly a motive for murder and it doesn't tie in with the missing drugs. Or does it?

Stanford and Franco are the first to emerge from their staterooms on the land yacht. "Time for a light lunch. I am famished. Holding a pit board is exhausting," Stanford announces. He opens the Sub-Zero double refrigerator doors and removes not one but two large trays filed with sandwiches he and Franco had obviously made just before the race session. Stanford then secures several bowls, covered with plastic wrap, which he ceremoniously removes and announces, "Fresh coleslaw, potato salad and a beet puree. To drink, we have several flavored waters, unsweetened iced tea and coffee, which you probably smell brewing."

I'll never again be able to face a peanut butter and jelly on white bread sandwich at the track.

"Let us all have a bite to eat. We have much to discuss. I want to especially thank Cecil who spent the better part of the morning doing his computer magic, rather than work on his race car." Margarite rises as she addresses the assembled.

"Nothing my dear. All in a day's work." Everyone chuckles, except Olivia and me who are still very much in the dark about what a *day's work* is to the Bentley Gang-plus one. "And I had invaluable help from Frederick and my dear brother."

"I am starved," the gallant Frenchman, who spent the morning with a beautiful car racing vocalist, announces. He is immediately booed and hissed.

CHAPTER THIRTY-TWO

After the luncheon is cleared, the big screen monitor displays a split image of Jung Kim. On one side of the screen is the rendering created by Charles from Don Montgomery's description and the other a passport looking photograph. I don't want to know where it came from. The screen changes and now we see an Asian male and female. "Bo-hyun Kim and Jai-hyun Kim," Cecil says. "Please note the family resemblance to one another but not to Jung Kim. Frederick, our resident linguist, noticed that both Bo and Jai use the family name *hyun,* but Jung does not. Our resources confirmed that Jung is the half brother of the others and younger by about fifteen years. It is said that when the mother of Bo and Jai died, their father *adopted* a younger woman, who subsequently became Jung's mother. In Korean culture, Jung's status was problematic, although his father acknowledged him. He is considered very smart, educated at Cal Tech, but somewhat hot headed. It is rumored that he was banished to South America after some kind of altercation in Korea. Details sketchy, but drugs cannot be ruled out."

I am getting a headache just thinking about the dots we need to connect. I sense Olivia is feeling the same.

"Cecil is building the dossier on the Kim family. Our contacts, so far, have not found any relationship between Costello, the murdered drug couriers and Kim," Hans is not shedding any light on the subject.

"May I ask a question?" I am seeking permission since we are really the outsiders.

"By all means, Thomas," Margarite answers. No question about the pecking order in this group.

"First of all, does anyone have the identity of the couriers and their place of origin?"

"Excellent question," Cecil retorts. "The deceased were carrying passports from . . ."

"Columbia?" I ask.

"And Argentina," Cecil continues. "We are trying to ascertain their itinerary immediately prior to their deaths. We know the shipment left Columbia and was transferred to the couriers stateside."

"I have made inquiry to ascertain if the Kim organization is involved in drugs independent of whatever involvement Jung may have. So far, they seem to be a typical conglomerate with tentacles in several high tech and telecommunication sectors and most recently, into the manufacture of performance tires. Drugs do not fit the image," Hans adds.

"Except Jung?" Olivia says.

"Possibly." Hans replies.

"We need to connect the couriers to Kim as their employer." Charles, who has heretofore not said anything, remarks. "I am still pondering the fact that Jung and young Montgomery's uncle were quarreling at a race track only two weeks ago and now Cosmo Costello is dead. I wish I had had the time to get a partial description of the second person with Jung."

"I have invited Don for dinner tonight. I'll ask him to come early."

"Not too early," Frederick inserts. "The Hudson has a race at 3:30."

"See what happens when the mechanic takes over. The Hudson has a race, but what about the driver?" Cecil's comment brings a few chuckles to the group.

"Hans, there doesn't seem to be any similarities in the manner of death between the two murders." Detective Nederfield asks.

"Basically both Costello and the couriers were killed at very close range. Other than that, nothing is similar. The attempt to disfigure the couriers to prevent identification was crude, ineffective and amateurish."

"Could it be Jung's handiwork?" I inquire.

"Of course no one is eliminated, but Jung Kim is a world class martial arts practitioner. Although he has been implicated in a number of physical altercations, in each case, the victim was beaten and kicked. No knife or other weapon was used. Whether he is an enforcer for Kim Enterprises or simply a violent personality, I am not sure."

Our attention is diverted by a knocking at the front door of the RV. Before anyone can move to answer, the door opens up and the *Marlboro Man* enters. From his snake skin cowboy boots to his black Stetson, the uninvited guest says *West Texas.*

"I'm so sorry y'all. I didn't mean to interrupt, but it's kind of an emergency."

"No problem William, please come in." Margarite is the only person, other than his mother, who ever called this rangy 6'4' man, *William.*

"Billie Ray, what is the problem?" Frederick asks.

"We need to borrow Charles," he drawls. "Hey, that's a picture of the guy from Kim tire," he continues.

Billie Ray a/k/a William has just blown everyone over with a proverbial feather.

"Yes, how do you know him?" I respond

"Kind of a long story but the other day all the Ford teams were given the opportunity to practice with the new engine and suspension specs. Being an independent team, Butch thought this was a great chance to try out our new package. You know, compare what we are doing with what the big guys are doing. We turned some pretty impressive laps and are convinced that when qualifying is wrapped up, we might grid the Mustang in the top ten or twelve. Well, no sooner have we gotten back to the garage, as that guy," pointing to Jung Kim's picture on the monitor, "comes in, wearing a suit, and starts in on me about switching to Kim tires. I didn't have time for the guy. Hell, I have the Mustang and the old Mercury to keep track of. I walk away. He then button holes Butch, who is itching to get out of his driver's suit and have a cold Dr. Pepper."

Olivia and I smile at each other. Our joke.

"This guy kind of gets up in Butch's face and says how much better his tires are than the Goodyear. Talks about temperature co-efficient and stuff like that. Says he'll pay to have us practice on Kim tires and compare. He claims the tires will eliminate one or maybe two tire changes in a long race because they wear so well with less heat build-up. Well Butch is listening, but also wanting to get rid of this guy. He gives the man, Mr. Taggert's card and says *he's the boss, you gotta talk to him.* The man nodded and left."

"Billie Ray, my name is Thomas Ballard . . ."

"I know who you are and I have been meaning to drop you a note thanking you for all those nice things you said about us small teams and how we keep the big teams honest and nipping at their hind quarters if they don't keep sharp."

"Thank you. Without you guys, there would only be fifteen cars on the grid instead of almost forty. You make it exciting. I do have a couple of questions for you about this man, whose name is Jung Kim. Was the man aggressive?"

"I think was a might pushy, but he was a salesman. Because I'm the crew chief, his type try to corner me all the time. I just send them to Mr. Taggert."

"Was he alone?"

"Actually there was another fellar with him. Didn't say a word. Just stood there."

"Can you describe him?"

"Come to think about it, he was pretty ordinary."

Charles reaches for his sketch pad and grabs a pencil and asks, "Can you describe the shape of his head?"

"Kind of regular. He wasn't Asian and was a bit taller than Kim. Dressed the same, except he wore an old fashioned hat."

"A fedora perhaps?" Franco, our resident fashion expert asks.

"Yeh. I remember my dad wearing one when we were kids. All the men wore them. The guy looked like one of those completely average men from old black and white movies. Nothing stands out. Sorry. I didn't pay much attention. Maybe you can ask Butch. Now that's the reason I came over in the first place. The Mercury kissed the wall this morning. We've got all the dings knocked out and she's sanded, primed and sanded again. We need Charles to spray her. Everything is masked and ready to go. The color may need a tweak but since it's white, it can't be too far off. We have the graphics ready to put on the door and rear fender once the paint sets up, but we've only got a couple of hours. Butch is so excited about being on the pole I am worried about him passing the pace car." Everyone chuckles.

"Did Rembrandt ever refuse such an offer," Charles quips. "Let's vamoose, Billie Ray."

CHAPTER THIRTY-THREE

"Now that was interesting, but I am not sure whether it was helpful," I muse.

"We know there was a second, heretofore unknown person with Jung Kim when he had his altercation with Cosmo Costello. Thomas, did you see anyone with Kim earlier this morning at the Goodyear trailer?" Hans is going somewhere, but I am not sure where.

"I didn't notice anyone but there might have been someone waiting in the ATV. Olivia?"

"May I put another spin on this?" Detective Nederfield asks but without waiting for an answer continues. "We know of three instances when Jung Kim has interacted with people we can identify. There is only one linkage between all three."

"Olivia, my dear, what do you discern as the common connection?" Margarite asks.

"Car racing," Olivia responds.

"What does Cosmo Costello have to do with . . . ?" I stop in mid sentence because my beautiful and brilliant companion is 100% correct.

"Excellent. Young Montgomery did not describe a physical confrontation, simply what appeared to be a heated discussion," Hans says.

"He never heard what they were saying, correct?" Stanford adds.

"Cosmo was the owner of Montgomery's car and his sponsor. The young driver was up and coming, but clearly on a budget. A tire deal might seem attractive. The exchange took place at a race track. Although Jung Kim's sales pitch is a bit animated, it does not rise to the level of murder," Olivia concludes.

"This disconnects dots rather than connects them," I observe.

"Franco, would you and Thomas go to the Goodyear trailer and speak with the fellow with whom Kim was arguing? I want to get as much information as possible about the subject matter of their chat. Pierre, can you enquire of the other drivers whether Kim has approached them about using his tires. Start with the vintage drivers here. Olivia, would you accompany Pierre. Your cover as a journalist may help and your powers of observation as a detective may also prove invaluable." Hans is on a roll. "Frederick and Cecil, I think it best if you begin your pre-race examination of the Hudson. I am assuming that you have enough on your plate Stanford, figuratively speaking of course, getting tonight's banquet organized. Margarite will reach out to our Asian contacts and I will contact some of our South American colleagues. Everyone back here at 3:00 to escort Team Hudson. We must make everything appear normal."

"Beau-frère. Brother-in-law, what shall we be looking for other than the obvious?" Pierre asks.

"Good question. We need to find a common thread. I am not satisfied that the motive for murdering Cosmo Costello and the couriers is the same. Nor am I satisfied that we have explored the Kim connection in sufficient depth."

"Do you think that there are two threads?" I ask.

"Maybe more," Olivia answers. "The motive for murder can always be found by pursuing the obvious: lust; love; loathing; or loot?"

"My vote is money," I volunteer. Everyone seems to agree.

"Selling tires does not seem like a very promising motive," Stanford says. "Unless . . ."

"What deviousness are you thinking?" Margarite asks.

"I am not satisfied that getting race car drivers to use Kim tires, or for that matter selling tire distributorships is the real issue. Manufacturing tires is contrary to Kim's core business; components for high tech applications. Even with government subsidies, why diversify so far? I do not want to discount drugs."

"Korean auto manufacturers have made a real dent in domestic as well as European and Asian markets," I offer.

"If every Korean manufactured car is using Kim tires, that's big business, but isn't the real money in after market?" Stanford continues.

"If Kim were to corner the small car performance tire market by producing a good product and being able to sell it for far less, then the business model makes sense," Olivia adds.

"I do not see murder in tires," Franco suggests.

"Nor do I," Hans responds, "And yet we do not know enough."

"I agree with Stanford that drugs should not be discounted," Frederick begins. "Remember the couriers had both Columbian and Argentinean passports and the Kim organization seems to be using Buenos Aires as its Western Hemisphere headquarters."

We all nod in agreement, although I am not sure what we are agreeing to.

"Hans, while we are on assignment, can you look into Henry Fuller and any connection he might have to Kim Enterprises?" I propose.

"Thomas, I read in your face something about Mr. Fuller," Margarite observes.

"It's just that his rise from washed up average second tier driver to race team owner is cloaked in secrecy. He simply has too much money, and based on my interaction with him, albeit years ago, I see red flags. Also, he seems very chummy with Juan Carlos Cidado. We have been focusing on the Kim family; maybe the Cidado branch needs a bit more scrutiny."

"Everything you say Thomas shall be done," Hans offers.

"Dépêchez-vous! Hurry up! We all have much to do." Margarite literally pushes us all out the door.

"Pierre, you had better be on your best behavior," I say as he and Olivia leave to interrogate helpless drivers. Olivia slips her arm into his and gives a little wave. It is comical since she is over six inches taller than Pierre. *C'est la vie.* I hook my arm into Franco's and we stroll off to see the Goodyear man. The waves of laughter behind us make me smile. Levity even in the face of death is a good thing.

CHAPTER THIRTY-FOUR

"Excuse me. I understand you have a very large person working here who had a conversation with a man named Jung Kim a couple of hours ago." I put on my nicest voice.

"What's it to you?" The rather surly young man replies.

"Sorry. My name is Thomas Ballard and I am doing a story on how certain brands of tires dominate certain segments of racing."

"Mister, write a letter to corporate. I don't have time."

"It's not your time I am interested in; it is the man who had the conversation." I breathe deeply before I punch this creep in the face or the back of the head since he turns and walks away. Time for plan B. "Hey kid!" I shout. "Turn around and take a look at this." I hold my deputy sheriff badge in front of his face and speed dial a number on my cell. "Sheriff, would you please send a marked car and a couple of uniforms over to the Goodyear rig at the track. I have a very uncooperative witness."

Franco raises an eyebrow.

"Thanks Josh." I push a button on the cell-the speaker phone. I want him to follow the unfolding events.

"Hey, I didn't know you were a cop," the youth stammers.

"Well now you know. Get the big guy . . . now!"

"Sure thing." He literally scampers off.

I pick up the cell. "Josh, this is getting complicated, but Cosmo's murder might have more to do with tires than cocaine."

"Thomas, what are you talking about?" Josh's voice does not need amplification.

"Can you come to the track first thing in the morning? I will have Hans arrange a briefing."

"Should Mike be in on the meeting? It's his jurisdiction." Mike is the Sheriff of Volusia County in which the track is located.

"No need. The only crimes we are investigating so far are a murder in Orange County and two murders in Miami-Dade County."

"What time?" Sheriff McCarthy asks.

Franco holds up eight fingers.

"Breakfast at 8 o'clock sharp. And I don't think we need back up. The guy we want to talk to is walking over toward us."

"My name is Danny O'Rourke and I am sorry about Bobby. He is a smart ass kid with a big mouth, but he is one of the best tire mounter we have ever had. What can I do for you gentlemen?" The man is truly of Paul Bunyan proportions.

"I happened to observe you and Jung Kim in what appeared to be a heated conversation this morning and I wondered if you could repeat what was said to me."

"Sure, but I am confused. The kid said you were a writer and then he said you were a cop."

"Actually both are true. My name is Thomas Ballard . . ."

"The car writer?"

"Yes. I am also a deputy sheriff and we are investigating a couple of incidents which may or may not relate to Jung Kim. I make it a point of not giving too much information to a go-between which is why I used my journalist identity."

"And who is your partner?"

"Buona sera. I am Franco." Franco opens his wallet and produces a laminated card. I try to catch a glance of who issued the ID, but Franco quickly returns it to his wallet. It certainly impressed Big Dan.

"I was changing some tires for the Thompson Toyota team when this guy shows up. He gives me his card which had his name and position as senior vice president of Kim Tires, Ltd. I knew that Kim tires is trying to get a foothold in the market, but couldn't figure out what it had to do with me. Well, he asked me if I would mount a set of his tires on some rims. I told him very politely that we could not mount tires not purchased through the Goodyear racing division. I have had to turn away some of the privateers who have been given or have bought used Goodyear race tires and I can't mount those either. This guy wasn't about to take no for an answer. I let him vent for a couple of minutes and then he gives up and walks back to his ATV with the tires in a trailer hitched to the back. I walk a little ways toward his rig to get a peek at the new Kim racing tire. It looked very cool with an asymmetric tread design. Not really tread but dimples in the rubber. I had heard that the Kim tire is supposed to perform as well as our tires, but last longer. That's it."

"Did you see anyone with Mr. Kim?"

"Come to think of it, there was this guy standing toward the back of the trailer with his arms folded. I remember him because he was wearing an old felt hat pulled down over his face like he was trying to get some shut eye. Other than that, there was nothing that stood out. He was real ordinary."

"Thanks for your time," I say and we start to walk away.

"Oh Danny, other than today, have you ever seen a Kim tire?" I ask.

"Not the racing kind. Some of guys who hang around the shop in Mooresville got a couple of sets of high performance street tires from some friends in California. They haven't really set up much of a distribution network on the East Coast yet. By the way, they really love the tires. Great traction, no side wall flex and a very aggressive tread design."

"Thanks again." This time we actually decide to leave.

"I wonder if Mr. Kim is only trying to set up dealers."

"I assume so." I don't want to appear terse but I sense that Franco has a thought.

"Kim tires are already being sold in South America, corretto?"

"Yes, but I still cannot connect the sale of Kim tires with murder and drugs."

"I do not either, but I am troubled by the fact that Kim Enterprises has gone so far from the source of its wealth; technology. I remember reading that the margin of profit is very small in tire sales and distribution, but very large in the sale and distribution of computer components. It does not, as you say, connect the dots."

As much as I respect Franco, what he says only adds another layer of confusion on an already confusing situation. If Kim tires are really good, why not diversify and corner a real hot market? If Jung Kim is not into drugs, I can't connect him to our investigation and it is easy to write off his argument with Cosmo as being less of an argument and more the way Jung Kim communicates.

"Let's head back and see how everyone else has done," I suggest.

"Molto buona."

CHAPTER THIRTY-FIVE

Our quest for information has yielded nothing of value. Let us assume that everyone concludes that Jung Kim is an obnoxious and overbearing tire salesman-so what? Franco does raise a good point about this being so far from the company's core business. Something upon which to ponder.

"Thomas, Franco, do you need something to drink? Perrier or your famous Gatorade?" Stanford is in a snappy mood.

"Grazie," Franco replies. "Just some water."

"Stanford, do you have any unsweetened iced tea?" I ask.

"Green tea or Earl Gray?"

"Wow! Iced Earl Gray sounds great. Thanks."

"Was your interview successful?" Hans asks as we enter the Ritz on wheels.

"Actually . . . no," I respond. "The Goodyear guy was helpful, but nothing he said helped."

"Thomas, you talk in riddles," Margarite observes.

"I mean he was cooperative and answered all our questions, but nothing he said added anything to our investigation."

"I am troubled," Franco inserts. "I do not understand why Kim Enterprises is interested in selling tires. It seems, how do you say, incongruent with everything I know about Asian business."

"I have been giving that some thought as well," Hans replies. "I have made some Level 2 inquiries about the Kim family and their businesses. Because of the time difference, I may not get a response for several hours."

I wonder what Level 2 means, but I am afraid to ask. Since both Franco and Stanford are nodding their heads, I think it is a big deal.

"Bon jour," Pierre says opening the door for Olivia to enter. He offers her a hand to navigate the stairs which is cute because of their respective height, but Gallic honor is unfazed by such trivial details.

"Merci," Olivia says.

"And how did y'all do?" I wanted to put a little southern touch in the conversation.

"The vintage drivers and their crews couldn't have been nicer, but they all said that they had not been approached by Kim. One very sweet gentleman enlightened me to the fact that the vintage rules dictate the size of the tires permitted as well as the compound and basic tread design, although there is no restriction concerning the manufacturer. Apparently the market is so small that only a few companies make the tires using old school molds." Olivia's presentation actually helps in that a lot of the participants are eliminated from our investigative consideration.

"Hans, have you gotten any feedback on Henry Fuller or the Cidado family?" I ask.

"Yes to the former and not yet to the latter, although I expect a very thorough report. The Argentinean police are very efficient, although a trifle slow. Your Henry Fuller is a very interesting person, although there are several gaps in my information. Born in Iowa in 1968, Mr. Fuller attended the local high school where he excelled at nothing, and then matriculated to Iowa State University where he dropped out after a year. Got a job as a mechanic for a small dirt track racing team and toured the Wisconsin, Illinois and Iowa circuit for a couple of years. Moved east and ended up in Georgia where he secured employment with another small short track team. Mr. Fuller got the opportunity to drive in a couple of races. By all accounts he was fast, but reckless."

I look at Olivia and nod.

"He was quite taken with himself and began self promoting. He was successful enough as a talker to find a sponsor and for about five years he actively participated on the late model circuit up and down the east coast. Henry Fuller would either win or crash, usually the latter. He was in an accident about twenty years ago for which he was suspended from racing. There was a fatality and talk of criminal prosecution. Mr. Fuller elected to hang up his helmet and relocate to Argentina where apparently extradition is somewhat difficult, especially when it involves motor racing. This is where the story is a bit . . . what do you say . . . fuzzy. I am waiting for more information. It appears that the paths of Juan Carlos Cidado's father, Georgio, and Henry Fuller, new expatriate, intersect about the same time Juan Carlos' mother passes away and Georgio marries Bo-hyun Kim."

"That is enough for now. We will know more when we return from the race. Gentlemen, please refresh your selves at the facilities provided by the track, while Olivia and I get ready here. Ten minutes." Margarite has spoken. We obey. As we exit, Franco hands us each a towel, tube of shower gel and a clean purple Hudson team shirt. He grabs a clothes bag and follows. This is the most efficient organization I have ever encountered.

I confess that a quick shower, with hot water, a rarity at most tracks, and a clean shirt makes one feel simply great. The ladies meet us at Cecil's car wearing matching white shirts with purple lettering. Charles has finished painting the Mercury and joins Frederick and his brother, each wearing matching fire suits.

Suddenly the public address system announces, "All vintage cars report to the false grid." The relative silence of the yellow garage area is shattered by the volcanic roar of forty engines coming to life. I long ago learned to wear ear plugs and have successfully trained Olivia to do the same.

Cecil wrestles the Hornet away from the trailer and toward the false grid. Below 10 miles per hour, the Hudson handles like a tank. If Margarite had had a whistle, we would have formed in single file. As it is, she leads us toward the pits. Franco carries his purple and white round sign on a pole and Stanford lugs the pit board. *HI HO, HI HO, it's off to race we go.*

CHAPTER THIRTY-SIX

Vintage stock car racing or for that matter any vintage racing, be it car, boat or plane, is definitely very cool. The cars each have a great history and reflect individuality both in terms of design and in terms of technology. Compared to modern stock cars, which cannot be distinguished one from the other except by the number on the side, hood or roof, the vintage competitors are each very different and instantly recognizable both in race livery or driving to the supermarket. Current rules attempt to make all racers *the same* so that spectators don't get bored and insure that no one make or model dominates. The old way was far better. Manufacturers employed new innovative designs into race cars which would later be incorporated into the cars your parents drove to work. And cars which utilized new technology did dominate until other manufacturers figured out ways to make their cars faster, handle better or brake better. That's the American way. If Dodge dominated one year it was because the car was simply better. The next year Ford would come up with something to make it more competitive.

The drivers were also a factor. Although in many respect they were not as athletic as today's fitness conscious racers, the good ol' boys knew a thing or two about throwing a two and a half ton monster around a corner. They were fearless and often engaged in a style more akin to bumper car than to high speed oval track racing. But it was part of the game. I think the demise of stock car racing is directly related to cost: cost to the manufacturers, many of which no longer exist, and to the teams. Getting sponsorship is more competitive than the actual on track racing. Think about it, only three companies participate at the highest level of stock car racing: Ford, Chevrolet and Toyota. Pontiac, Oldsmobile, Mercury, Hudson, Studebaker, Plymouth and Chrysler are not even produced any more. Dodge and Buick don't compete. I have a right to be nostalgic.

Butch's white Mercury, sporting Charles' new paint job, did not yield its pole position until a winged ex-Richard Petty Superbird Plymouth uses its aerodynamic advantage (and a few horse power) to out drag the Merc to the checker. Cecil's Hudson Hornet finishes a respectable fifth, which considering it was gridded at the back of the pack because of his finishing position in the morning, was quite a good drive. Based on the smiles all around and the standing ovation from the crowd for all the competitors, the race was a rip roaring success.

Climbing down from our crew chief perch, Margarite says, "Let's check to see if any of our contacts have replied to our enquiries. Frederick, Charles and Cecil can put away the Hornet for the evening. Franco and Stanford have to put the finishing touches on our banquet."

"Thomas, you mentioned that you invited young Montgomery to dinner, yes?" Hans asks.

"Yes. I hope you don't mind."

"No, to the contrary. I am considering extending an invitation to Juan Carlos Cidado and your Henry Fuller," Hans replies.

"He is not *my* Henry Fuller. I release all claims." Olivia, Margarite and Hans all smile.

"Thomas, you are a fair weather friend after all," Olivia adds.

"Maybe I can give him to Goodwill as a charitable deduction," I quip.

"Let us see what our people find out about Mr. Fuller before we give him away." Hans winks and wraps his arm around Margarite's waist. I do the same to Olivia, who doesn't punch me for a change.

"If it is okay with you folks, I want to make a quick detour and drop in on Don Montgomery. I know he had a practice session this afternoon and I want to see how he is holding up. And it gives me a chance to repeat the dinner invitation." It's a little strange that I feel like I have to ask permission.

"Splendid idea," Margarite responds.

Olivia gives my arm a squeeze and my cheek a quick kiss.

"If you cross paths with either Juan Carlos or Henry Fuller, ask them to join us at 6:30 for cocktails, followed by what I trust will be a fabulous meal." I am learning to read Hans' *between the lines* meanings. In this case he is asking us to find the two aforementioned individuals and get them to join us.

"I am more than a little curious about Fuller's relationship with Cidado the elder. What could they possibly have in common and how does the former Ms Kim fit into the picture?" Detective Nederfield has been ruminating for a while.

"My lovely and most charming companion, I suspect the network of Hans Leiter will disclose everything in time. Let's check in on young Montgomery and track down Juan Carlos and Fuller. Maybe we should invite Jung Kim as well, he's practically family."

"What are you talking about Thomas?"

"Jung Kim is Juan Carlos' step uncle."

"Quite true, however for the sake of Stanford and Franco, who have been slaving away over a hot stove, until we can connect more dots, let's leave Mr. Kim out. Anyway, he might not like what's being prepared anyway."

"Yeh, and don't forget the guy in the felt hat." My comment brings out that special Olivia Nederfield smile. I put my arm around her waist. She puts her head on my shoulder, which is quite a feat since we are both over six feet tall. I could get used to this.

My moment of serenity comes to a halt when the public address system announces that qualifying for the Trophy series-stock car racing's crème de la crème-is about to begin. The session is formatted so that five cars are on the track at the same time for six laps: two warm up and four at speed. Because of the size of the grid, there will be eight sessions. The groups are selected by a random draw. I think that the procedure has less to do with safety than showmanship. The top drivers are scattered throughout the sessions, keeping spectators in their seats. Normally I would watch qualifying, but I have other errands to complete. Then it occurs to me that Juan Carlos may be driving one of Henry Fuller's cars, thus both will be in the same place at the same time.

"I think we should check out the timed session since both Cidado and Fuller will be there," Olivia says. I wonder if my mind is that easy to read.

"Good idea. I hadn't thought of that." Not!

We quick march over to the pits. Our press credentials allow immediate and total access. Some of the drivers are milling around until their turn on the track. Media, particularly social media, have made many of the better known drivers virtual movie stars and even some of the lesser known drivers are actually recognizable outside of their cars. I spy Butch and his crew chief Billie Ray in an intense discussion standing next to their number 66 Mustang. Campaigning as an independent is really difficult, but I think that their team employs some of that old school innovative spirit which makes the factory teams give them respect. After the performance he and the old Mercury put on during the vintage race, I bet Butch is ready to go.

The first two rounds of qualifying are completed without a hitch. The third session is marred by a rather nasty accident. A Camaro owned by none other than Henry Fuller hits the wall at full force coming out of turn three. Fortunately the car stays upright although one can see daylight under all four tires for an instant. The track is littered with debris and the qualifying session is red flagged. All the cars slow to school zone speed and enter the pit lane in single file. The emergency crew arrives at the crash site almost instantly. After a rather breath holding couple of minutes, the driver slowly gets out of the wreck.

"Is that Juan Carlos?" Olivia asks.

"I can't tell. Let's put our journalistic talents to work. If it is Juan Carlos, I would like to an interview with both driver and owner." When you're a member of the fourth estate, it's in your blood.

The safety crew loads the obviously shaken driver into the ambulance and proceeds to the medical area, while a flatbed tow truck is dispatched to pick up the Camaro or what's left of it. The bodies on the new cars are so flimsy looking that a minor wreck appears far worse.

"Olivia, do you see Henry Fuller high tailing it to the medical area?"

"Yes. Let's get through this mob and try to corner him before the driver is released."

We lose sight of Henry when the tow truck moves up the pit lane toward the garage area. He reappears and engages several crew members with wild gyrations, one of whom raises his hand to stop the wrecker. He walks over to the right side of the car, which is rather mangled, and stares at the front tire. He beckons Henry and several other crew members, all of whom quickly move to the right front of the car. We speed up hoping to hear some of their conversation or at least look at the right front tire of the wrecked race car. Olivia is thinking exactly the same thing as she removes her cell phone from her pocketbook.

"I think we should take some photos before whatever it is that is causing such an explosion of rather colorful language from the otherwise taciturn Henry Fuller disappears."

"Whatever he is looking at is really got him upset. Let's hustle."

CHAPTER THIRTY-SEVEN

We circle around the tow truck. Olivia is trying to position herself so that she can take some pictures of the tire. In order to get Henry's attention, I say, "Looks like the tire went flat."

"The infatigable Thomas Ballard and his gorgeous companion are already on the scene to get first hand news."

"Henry, you wouldn't have it any other way. How's Juan Carlos?"

"A little rattled, but okay. The medicos are still checking him out but he texted me a couple of minutes ago."

"What happened? He looked pretty good out there."

"Thomas, take a look at this. And the lovely Miss Olivia." Henry Fuller's performance is worthy of an academy award. The back of his neck is still red and I can tell he is seething.

And I see why. A screw has obviously been driven into the side wall of the tire and then some with kind of black goop smeared over the head so that is not immediately obvious.

"The kid is lucky the tire went down slowly. If it had blown, he might not have had the Safer barrier to slow him down. Any ideas?" I suspect Henry is still getting over the shock.

"This is not for publishing Thomas, but a lot of weird things have been happening the last several weekends. We have always been the smallish, understated team. Our cars are competitive but we have yet to find the right combination of driver and machine. That is why I was trying out Juan Carlos. He seems to have the knack. I knew his father in Argentina and have watched him mature as a driver."

Suddenly, Fuller stops. "Are you okay?" I ask.

"I'm fine. The car can be fixed, the driver is not hurt and the sun is shining." Henry has become flippant.

"What about the weird things you mentioned?"

"Nothing but a little bad luck."

"Henry, having someone drive a screw into the tire of your race car is hardly bad luck."

"Must have picked it up from the garage floor. Just bad luck."

Olivia, who has been listening changes subjects completely and asks, "If you and Juan Carlos are up to it, we have having a dinner at the yellow garages with cocktails at 6:30 and we would like you to come."

"That is very nice. I want to see how the kid feels. His uncle is around somewhere and he may want Juan Carlos to rest."

"His uncle?" Olivia asks knowing full well that Fuller is referring to Jung Kim.

"Actually his father's wife's brother. He's kind of looking out for the kid."

"Understood. There's always room at the bar if you decide to join us," Olivia replies.

"Cheers." Henry Fuller starts to move away from both the car and us.

I discreetly rub my finger over the black substance covering the screw. I sniff the goop. The smell is unique. Not automotive. "What do you think?" I ask Olivia.

She grabs my finger to give it the sniff test. "It is definitely not petrochemical. It actually smells like rotten guava or mango."

I withdraw my finger and smell. "Yuck. It is disgusting and although I can't identify the source, it is clearly organic. This was no accident."

"I am going to send the pictures back to Hans. Let's poke around a bit."

I am not sure what we are looking for, but it strikes me that when I see it, I'll recognize it. Whatever that means. The tow truck drags the smashed car back to the garage area. I suspect that Henry Fuller's team has at least one spare car that can be made race ready in a couple of hours. Actually, Juan Carlos' car looks to be more superficially damaged than structural and might be fixable by tomorrow.

"Let's head over to the medical area and talk to Juan Carlos before he has a chance to process the fact that his car was sabotaged by person or persons unknown for reason or reasons also unknown." Olivia could have said all that in about five words.

"After we chat with Juan Carlos, I want to check out the team's tire guy," I suggest.

"Thomas, aren't the tires used in qualifying different from those used in the race?"

"Very often that is true. Daytona is a track that allows the use of special tires for qualifying."

"This would mean the tires are somehow designated differently so they don't get mixed up. And that would be the tire guy's responsibility. I think we need to pay him a visit." Detective Nederfield is on a roll.

"Let's talk with Juan Carlos now. The tire guy isn't going anywhere."

"Vamonos!"

"Show off."

We scurry off, hand in hand to the medical center where we are greeted by a very large and very authoritarian medic, who is totally unimpressed with my press credentials, but quite impressed when we showed him our badges. I think Olivia was going to retrieve her Glock from her immense purse if necessary. He even opens the door for us.

The medical center at a track is rather much like the nurse's office in an elementary school. Clean, efficient and simple. If anything is really wrong with a driver they are either rushed by ambulance to the closest hospital or heaven forbid-air lifted. A paramedic opens the privacy screen just as we enter. Juan Carlos doesn't look worse for wear.

"Buenas tardes," Olivia says. "Cómo estás?"

"Muy bien. Gracias."

"What happened out there?" I ask.

"It was quite strange. The first lap was very good. I was holding my line and the car was running perfecto. Then on the second lap, coming out of turn three, it felt like something was pushing the front of the car up toward the wall. I tried to correct but the Mustang just kept climbing toward the top. I knew I was going to hit so I took my hands off the steering wheel and folded my arms across my chest. Then bang. I was, how do you say, shaken . . . not stirred." Juan Carlos chuckles at his own joke. "I hope Mr. Fuller is not mad at me."

"I don't think anyone considers the accident your fault. It appears there was some kind of problem with the tire. I am sure your crew chief will explain everything. If you feel better, join us for dinner in the yellow garages at 6:30. You may be a little bruised, but I am glad you are okay."

"Gracias Mr. Ballard. At 6:30 then. Adiós."

We take our leave.

"Let's drop in on Don Montgomery," I suggest.

"Good idea. I want to think about things for a while. Tomorrow morning we should pay the tire guy a visit. Maybe talk to Danny at Goodyear."

"I agree. We really should sleep on it." My comment is greeted with a punch in the shoulder.

"Dirty old man."

I simply shrug.

CHAPTER THIRTY-EIGHT

The one thing about race weekend at Daytona is the precision with which practices, qualifying and races are scheduled, most of which is thrown out the window after the first red flag or the first lightning strike, which in Central Florida, the lightning capital of the world, is frequent. It is not altogether surprising when lightning strikes at the rate of 1,000 per hour. That's a lot of electricity and thus NASCAR has a rule that on track activities will be suspended for thirty minutes from the last strike within eight miles of the track. We have been lucky so far today, but Friday's forecast is a bit iffy.

We catch Don Montgomery returning from the showers after his qualifying, terry cloth towel and all. I place my hands over Olivia's eyes. She promptly pries my fingers off with entirely more force than is necessary. The young driver does not seem overly embarrassed.

"Sorry. At UCF we have co-ed showers and it gets a little informal."

"No problem. We just want to make sure we are on for 6:00 and check how practice went," I say.

"Thanks for asking. I wasn't sure how I'd feel so I called a couple of college buddies to come over and be my pit crew.

They were a great help, mostly just being there and I actually ran the third fastest qualifying time. I am psyched for tomorrow's 40 lap qualifying race. The car is running really well."

"See you in a bit," Olivia adds.

"What is the proper attire?" It is refreshing when a kid actually asks what he should wear.

"I suggest a collared polo shirt and either shorts or chinos, although it may chill off quite early this evening," I add.

"Uncle Cosmo had some cool team shirts made up. I'll wear one in his honor." Young Montgomery chokes up a little.

"Perfect. TTFN." We walk away.

"TTFN?" Olivia asks.

"But of course."

"Explain yourself bard of the race track.

"TA TA FOR NOW. TTFN." I wonder why Olivia looks at me as if I have three heads.

"Let's see what Hans has discovered from his sources."

"Splendid idea." We head back toward the yellow garages.

"Excuse me!" A man screams as he races across the parking lot.

"Can we help you?" Detective Nederfield asks in her law enforcement voice.

"Yes." The man is trying to catch his breath. "Mr. Fuller asked me to find you to say that something has come up and he won't be able to join you for dinner tonight but would like to meet you both in the owner's lounge at ten in the morning for a bite to eat. Oh, and Juan Carlos can't come for dinner either. The doctors want him to rest. He has to go back to the medical people tomorrow morning before he can be cleared to race."

"Thank you. Please tell Mr. Fuller that Mr. Ballard and I will join him in the morning and if you see Juan Carlos that we hope he feels better. TTFN."

The man stares at Olivia for an instant, shakes his head and starts to walk back to-where ever.

"I can't believe you," I sputter.

"If you can say stupid things, so can I." Olivia sticks out her tongue at me but grabs my hand and starts to march.

Should I whistle *Bridge over the River Kwai?*

On track activities are slowing down. The truck guys have wrapped up their first qualifying session without a major wreck and a quick glance at my foix Rolex says that it is almost 5 o'clock already. Time flies when you are having fun. The organizers try to end racing early on Thursday so that the track cleaning equipment can do their thing without the necessity of turning on the lights. We must be cost conscious.

"I am glad that Fuller and Juan Carlos bailed on tonight. There are too many things to think about without being distracted, although each is definitely worth closer scrutiny," Detective Nederfield reflects.

"Yup." When you have nothing to add-don't.

"I wonder what's for dinner." Olivia is tactfully changing the subject to one which will certainly get my attention.

"Whatever it is, I am sure it will be fantastic. Other than the cuisine and a cold beer, I think we should bring our young driver up to speed," I add.

"We have time to quickly go over Hans' findings, take yet another shower and meet up with Montgomery at 6:00." Olivia is always perfectly coiffed, even after busting some hoodlum. Appearance is everything.

With the end of racing, the noise level drops to a point where two people can have a normal conversation, although talking about triple homicides is hardly normal-except for us. I grab hold of Olivia's hand, as much for me as for her. We have a long journey ahead, but we have great folks to travel with.

I want to say something deep and meaningful but instead ask, "Do you think Franco washes the team shirts at the track or does he simply bring a dozen or so for each of us?"

"Thomas, what would cause you to express such a deep and meaningful thought?"

The thought that Olivia can read my mind is scary, but also refreshing. Scary because I don't even know what I am thinking sometimes. Refreshing because it means we are connected in some very surreal way. I guess being around the Bentley Seven has allowed me to understand the importance of subliminal communication. It works so well for them. Maybe it's rubbing off. I hope some of their self fulfillment and mutual respect also wears off. We could use a little more of that in the world. I lean over and give Olivia Nederfield, my beloved, a kiss.

CHAPTER THIRTY-NINE

As we have come to expect, Stanford has several chilled liquid refreshments awaiting-both non-alcoholic and alcoholic. Olivia and I select the former assuming that there will be plenty of beer and wine at dinner. And besides, I have a couple of questions for Hans and Margarite about Henry Fuller and his connection with the Cidado family.

"Our message bearers have returned," Charles announces. "Did you confirm our meeting with young Montgomery? I really want to try to get an image of the mysterious man with Jung Kim."

"He will be here at six but unfortunately neither Juan Carlos nor Mr. Fuller will be in attendance," I reply.

"I trust you have a theory about their declination of our invitation," Hans offers.

"Yes . . . and no," Olivia adds. "Juan Carlos had a rather nasty crash during qualifying and although he initially accepted, the doctors told him to rest."

"Probably wise. Is he injured?" Margarite asks.

"Bumps and bruises. The Safer barrier did its job and absorbed most of the impact," I answer. "However the cause of the accident seems to be rather suspicious. A screw was found in the sidewall of his right front tire."

"Incidente?" Franco asks.

"Neither of us thinks so. We found this substance smeared over the head of the screw to make it less visible." I retrieve the plastic bag with the smelly stuff and hand it to Charles who has thrust his hand, palm up, toward me. He opens the bag and smells the contents.

"It is very ripe avocado. The natural oil will keep it adhered to the surface to which it was applied."

"Charles, can you tell us the source?" Olivia is got e bee in her bonnet.

"Let me smell," Chef Stanford says. He not only smells the goop but places a dab on his tongue. "It is not a native Florida avocado. It is a Hass and is either from the southern portion of California or from Mexico."

This type of information would take the average crime lab a week to secure, if they were actually able to do so. It takes the Bentley Seven maybe three minutes. Amazing, but of what value does the type of avocado have in the investigation?

"Is there anything you can glean from that?" Olivia once again reads my mind.

"But of course, my dear Detective Nederfield. Hass avocados are not locally available at his time of year, so I deduce that whoever put the substance on the screw purchased the avocado near its place or origin: most likely Mexico." Stanford sounds like Sherlock Holmes addressing Dr. Watson.

"Olivia . . . Thomas is it possible that the screw pierced the tire as a result of an accident, as Franco asked? Maybe the tire fell onto the screw." Hans is not yet wrapping his arms around the sabotage theory.

"The screw was driven into the tire by a force far greater than a rim and tire falling. It was intentionally obscured. What I am asking myself is *was it a warning?* If so, who was being warned: Fuller or Cidado?" Looking around the assembled team, I swear I hear wheels churning-the mental kind.

"May I make a suggestion?" Margarite tends to make a statement into a question. It is more polite. "We are still waiting for information on the Kim family, the Cidado family, the Costello family and Henry Fuller. Our sources are a bit slow, but we have been assured that they are being extremely thorough. Let's all get ready for cocktails and dinner and a chat with Donald Montgomery. The schedule for tomorrow allows a little more time for investigating. Cecil has his feature races both Friday and Saturday in the afternoon and an exhibition parade on Sunday at noon. It has been reported that the car is running *à la perfection, est-ce exact?"*

"Oui," Cecil and Frederick answer together.

"Très bon. Then we will have much time to, how do you say, get to the bottom of this. I think that we need to spend time considering options and then we can all share our thoughts. *N'est pas?"* Mother Superior has spoken.

"Thomas and I are going over to Nellie Belle and freshen up. We will be back at 6." Olivia has spoken.

"Nellie Belle?" Charles asks.

"Olivia gave the Airstream a nick name," I answer. Charles shakes his head in that way reserved for bachelors.

"Per favore. Can you bring me your dirty shirts when you return? I need to launder all the uniforms tonight." Franco hands me a mesh bag.

I feel a sharp elbow in my ribs.

"Also, if you have anything else that needs cleaning, just put it in the bag."

We take our leave and stroll over to Nellie Belle. Olivia neither punches me nor sticks out her tongue, but does say, "I think that a quick shower will wash off the grime of the day. Somehow I feel grubby."

"Hanging around Henry Fuller will do that. Speaking of which, isn't that the kid who told us neither Juan Carlos or Fuller would be coming tonight?"

"And he's got ants in his pants," Olivia observes.

The young man is frantically waiving while shouting, "Mr. Ballard! Come quickly."

"Slow down. Where should we go and why?"

"There's been a terrible accident at Mr. Fuller's garage. Harvey's hurt real bad. I think he is dead." The young man's voice quivers.

"Who is Harvey and what happened?"

"Harvey is the tire guy. It looks like he was hit on the head by a tire iron. As soon as I saw him, I rushed out to find you. Mr. Fuller is already gone and I couldn't think of who else to tell."

"Okay, let's go." I am not sure why Fuller's crew man didn't notify security, but he seems so shaken, clear thinking is not high on his list.

"Thomas, we need to make a call first." Olivia is absolutely correct.

I pull out my cell phone and speed dial. "Josh, just listen. There's been a murder or at least an attempted murder. We are going over to see the victim. You need to call Mike and have him get a medical unit out here pronto. I expect he'll want to send at least one car. Please make it unmarked and no sirens. This may tie into the investigation. I don't have time to explain. Give Mike my number. Team Fuller garage.

Olivia and I will be there and secure the scene." I push the end button.

"I think we should call Hans," Olivia suggests.

"On the way there. Let's hustle. I don't want any rubberneckers."

We start to jog. I am glad we have been putting in the miles each morning. The crew guy, who is no older than 25, is panting. Olivia is multi tasking. I can't believe that she can keep up the pace, while talking in a perfectly calm voice to Hans.

"Hans is bringing Frederick and Cecil to help secure the site. Charles is going to photograph and then get back by 6 to meet with Don Montgomery. Stanford is already slowing down dinner preparations."

Now it's my time to multi task. I answer my cell. Mostly I listen. "See you in fifteen minutes," I say to the caller.

"Who was that?" Olivia asks.

"Sheriff Mike. Josh gave him the low down and he is on his way over. He understands that this is important, but low key." Mike Wetherford is the Volusia County Sheriff. He is also a full blooded Seminole who grew up in the Everglades. He is tough, smart and totally no nonsense.

CHAPTER FORTY

We arrive about a nanosecond before Franco skids to a halt in the Team Bentley all purpose golf cart. It doesn't take long to find the tire man. He is lying in a pool of blood next to a pile of tires, with a nasty gash on his forehead and a heavy steel bar next to him. I check. No pulse. Charles quickly sets up his camera gear while Franco and Cecil unwind yellow crime scene tape although it says *CAUTION—GAS LEAK.*

"It draws far less attention and keeps crowds away. Police tape is like a magnet, but nobody cares about leaking gas, except to stay away," Cecil explains.

Fuller's crew guy finally catches his breath. "Is he dead?"

"I am afraid so and I am going to have to ask you to stand over there and wait until we call you," I say.

"Yes sir!"

Hans is moving around the body with practiced efficiency. He measures the ambient temperature as well as the temperature of the deceased tire man, Harvey. Cecil has already opened a tablet and walks toward the young crew member.

"Do you know Harvey's full name and any other information about him?"

"Are you a policeman?"

"Yes he is and so are all these other folks," a voice as deep as a cavern says.

The voice belongs to a man wearing a checked shirt with his long black hair pulled back into a pony tail. The gold badge at his waist identifies Sheriff Mike. "Deputy Ballard and Detective Nederfield, how nice to see you again, although I wish the circumstances were a bit more cheery. Josh told me not to be surprised when I got here and that you had some colleagues working with you and that I shouldn't ask. It is clear that you have already secured the perimeter and started forensics. The M.E. will be here in about 10 minutes. I am a bit curious about the crime tape."

"Buona sera. I am Franco. Charles is taking photographs, Hans is checking temperature, Cecil is talking to the young man who notified Olivia and Thomas of the *incidente* and I am responsible for the yellow tape. We have found that it causes people to leave the scene we are examining rather than coming closer."

Sheriff Mike leans back and starts to laugh. "Josh was right. Don't ask."

Hans approaches the Sheriff. "My name is Hans Leiter. The time of death is between 3 and 4 pm. I cannot be more specific because the concrete floor cools at a different rate that most surfaces and I have not yet entered that data into my program . . . but I will shortly. Charles has taken every possibly photograph without moving the decedent or any potential evidence. The cause of death appears to be blunt force trauma, but I will leave that to your medical examiner to determine. As soon as you give me permission I will be dusting for fingerprints on the apparent weapon and other obvious surfaces. I will send whatever prints I can scan to the appropriate agencies for identification. Sometimes your local databases are better able to identify prints from items like fishing licenses, gun permits and minor traffic offenses."

"We were taught at a very young age to respect our elders who we were told are much wiser. You have whatever permission you need to do whatever you think is necessary."

"Thank you Sheriff Wetherford. We will try to be efficient and not underfoot." Hans excuses himself and returns to retrieve fingerprints-I guess.

"How did he know my name?" Sheriff Mike asks no one in particular.

"Don't ask!" Olivia and I answer in tandem. "Sheriff, if what happened here connects to what we have been looking into, this is way over our pay grade."

"Josh's overview was a bit skimpy."

"Before I forget, now that you are part of the investigative group since this is your jurisdiction, we are having a meeting at 8 o'clock tomorrow morning at the yellow garages to go over what we have learned. As we speak several members of the group are connecting with sources all over the world."

"You are kidding, right?"

Cecil approaches and says, "Hello I am Cecil Llewellyn and that chap over there is my brother Charles."

"The famous photographer?"

"Actually, he is rather well known and I have to admit that he does good work. In any event, I think I have an ID on the deceased; Harvey Silver, born in Charlotte on January 10, 1989. He came to work for Henry Fuller about three years ago as an expert in racing tires after learning his trade with Haskell Racing. I have sent his bio to our regular sources to get his prints which we can compare with whatever Hans secures. I have also asked for the prints of the young man,

Ricky Nielson, who found the body, as well as those of several of the crew members. I thought we should also have the prints of Mr. Fuller and young Cidado."

Sheriff Mike turns to us and says, "Don't ask."

A Volusia County Fire and Rescue vehicle pulls up to the garage, and a rather tired looking man exits. His suit looks like he slept in it. And who wears a suit in Florida anyway?

After brief introductions, the medical examiner walks over to Hans. They speak for several minutes, frequently referring to Hans' tablet. The doctor kneels over the corpse and gently turns it, formerly him, over. Charles immediately begins photographing. Hans puts on a pair of surgical gloves and raises the dead tire man's hand, lifting each finger, which he rolls onto a sheet of clear plastic.

"I will email you the thermal readout. I have examined the apparent murder weapon for fingerprints, but I did not take tissue or blood samples from the tire tool or the decedent. I assume you will be performing a standard autopsy." Hans says.

Before the M.E. answers, the Sheriff says to him, "Richard, all these folks are part of different segments of the law enforcement community and I have promised them complete cooperation."

"Sheriff, you misunderstood my hesitation. I was going to ask whether this gentleman had my email address. It is obvious that he is trained in forensic pathology and possesses knowledge and uses instrumentation that is seldom seen outside of a highly funded medical school laboratory."

"Thank you for your kind word words, doctor. I do have your email addresses. Shall I send my findings to your office or to your personal address or both?"

"How did you get my personal email address?"

"Richard, I just met these folks and have adopted the operative words: *don't ask.*" I am glad Sheriff Wetherford is doing the explanation this time. "Within five minutes of arriving at the scene, they had secured the perimeter, interviewed the person who found the victim, identified the victim, sent off requests for background information and have begun a forensic investigation including pictures by a world renowned photographer. I think I've got everything. Detective Nederfield, did I leave anything out?"

Before Olivia can reply, Stanford and Pierre arrive in the other golf cart. "I've got everything under control at headquarters, so Margarite thought you might want some refreshment. I have quite a selection in the cooler. Don't worry, there's nothing alcoholic Sheriff Wetherford. Oh, I'm Stanford and this fellow who came along for the ride is Pierre."

"Bon jour. My sister wants me to return Charles to the RV so he can meet with Monsieur Don at 6."

"Sheriff, are there any other pictures of the crime scene or decedent you wish me to take before I leave?" Charles asks.

"Do you have everything you need?" Sheriff Mike replies.

"I do. I will email the contact sheets to you and to the medical examiner's office. I can enhance any image you wish."

"It's getting late, so maybe it would be best to send them to my personal email address."

"It'll be within the hour." Charles picks up his gear and slides onto the seat of the cart. Stanford has removed the cooler and is ready to serve.

"Cecil, you need to drink some water," Charles says in departure.

The medical examiner is speechless. I think the Sheriff is as well. Olivia calls out to Cecil, "With or without gas?"

It takes a second for the play on words to catch on. Here we are in a NASCAR garage with a corpse and Olivia is asking whether Cecil wants carbonated water or plain.

"Do you have any of that splendid lime Gatorade? I am parched."

No wonder. Lest we forget, Cecil had two track sessions today.

CHAPTER FORTY-ONE

In short order, Harvey is placed into the rescue truck and taken to where ever medical examiners do whatever medical examiners do.

"Sheriff, we have gone through the garage several times and I haven't found anything else remotely related to the murder. I did expand my search to the garage next door."

"Why?"

"I am glad you asked." Olivia smiles at my cat and mouse game. "In the stall next door you will find a rather worse for wear number 31 Camaro. It hit the wall during qualifying. It also had a screw embedded into the sidewall of the right front tire. It was also driven by Juan Carlos Cidado, son of the Kim tire distributor in the Americas, who is a business associate of team owner Henry Fuller."

"That is about as clear as the 'Glades on a foggy morning." Sheriff Mike uses a son good ole' boy cliché.

"There is a lot more here than meets the eye and after joining us for our morning get together, all these disparate facts will be connected." Detective Nederfield to the rescue. "Thomas, did you find the damaged tire?"

"The car is jacked up and all four tires have been removed. And they are not readily visible. I think we should clean up here and let Hans and Cecil send off requests for data. I am also suggesting that a couple of Volusia plain clothes deputies plan to spend the night in this garage and the one next door. I have a sneaking feeling that someone may want to return to the scene of the crime or actually next door to the scene of the crime. We can't ask the tire man *what happened to the practice tires,* can we?"

"We can, but I think the conversation would be a trifle one sided." Sheriff Mike shows a sense of humor.

"Everyone ready to go?" Cecil asks. "Sheriff Wetherford, can one of your deputies locate the persons on this list and get their finger prints?"

"Where do you think these folks can be found?"

"I ran a quick search and each has a residential address in and around Mooresville, North Carolina so I assume they are staying either at the track or in a motel nearby. Ricky Neilson said that most of the guys on the crew are older and have worked and partied together for years. They usually stay at a place at the beach on old Route 1. Sheriff, I texted you pictures of the crew from their driver's licenses. It might help locating the men. I will try a somewhat back door approach to get the fingerprints as well."

Sheriff Wetherford's cell phone starts to vibrate. "I'm glad we are all on the same team. You guys are creepy and I won't ask how you got my cell phone number." He opens his phone and begins to scroll. "This will certainly help. Mr. Leiter, is there anything else you need?"

"I think I have everything for now."

Stanford hands the Sheriff a bottle of Perrier. "It quenches one's thirst."

We load everyone and everything into the golf cart, except Olivia and *moi.* We walk.

"You look troubled," I observe.

"In my experience, killers usually stick with a single *modus operandi.* You know; knives, guns, poison, that sort of thing. The gun and knife murders don't seem connected. Jung Kim, who is an on again off again suspect, probably would have broken Harvey's neck. A heavy steel bar is often a weapon of spontaneity."

"That opens a can of worms. Are you suggesting that his death might not have anything to do with our investigation?" I am no more enlightened than I was a couple of hours ago.

"Thomas, since we do not believe in coincidences, let me pose the following possibility. Harvey the tire guy had been instructed to remove and examine the tires."

"By whom?"

"Not so fast. Just listen. There are three reasons why he might have been told to take off the tires; routine removal so that the crew can work on the chassis and repair the damage; removal to examine the tires, especially the right front; and thirdly, removal to get rid of the tires."

"Okay, now what?"

"Let's assume Harvey was simply told to remove the wheels and tires. Who could give him that order?"

"The crew chief most likely," I answer. "Wait! Henry Fuller!"

"Who we know was around the garage at the time, although young Neilson said he had gone. I suspect that the body was discovered after Fuller left the garage area. Remember that Fuller cancelled dinner because something had suddenly come up. But what motive?"

"I think that Mr. Team Owner was as surprised as we were when he saw the screw in the tire sidewall and pretty angry."

I am not getting good vibes. "Olivia, unless something really bizarre is going on, I can't see Fuller whacking Harvey. I can see him going after whomever he thought tried to wreck the car, unless there was something that implicated Harvey."

"Someone had something to do with the damaged tire. Right?" Detective Nederfield asks rhetorically. "That someone could either have put the screw in the tire or had someone do it. That someone must have been pretty pissed at Fuller."

"My dear Olivia, what if Henry wasn't the intended subject, but Juan Carlos?"

"The step son of the sister of the head of Kim Enterprises."

"Somewhat far afield," I observe

"Yes, but we do not yet know the nature of the relationship between Señor Cidado the elder and Fuller."

"I feel a migraine coming on."

"Me, too. Motive . . . motive . . . motive. Thomas, let's head back to the RV and have a cold beer and enjoy whatever dinner Stanford has created. I am all washed up for the day."

"Gee I was hoping to share a shower with you later on." My comment gets an expected response-a punch in the arm.

CHAPTER FORTY-TWO

The psychic power of the Bentley Seven (plus one) is amazing. As we approach the team hotel on wheels, Franco rushes toward us. "A Peroni beer for each of you. Ice cold." Our omnipresent co-host hands us each a bottle, safely wrapped in a British racing green koozie with the mandatory yellow B. A koozie for those who live in cold climes is a foam sleeve that insulates a bottle or can-keeping the temperature at a perfect 50 degrees Fahrenheit. "Margarite has said that there will be no discussion of the case tonight."

"The beer is *perfezionare.* Absolutely what I needed," Olivia purrs with appreciation.

"Grazie," I say and take a deep swig. "Has Donald Montgomery arrived?"

"Sì. I am afraid even Charles could not draw the other person with Jung Kim. The young man's description was too *vago* . . . vague."

"I am starved and looking forward to one of Stanford's creations," Olivia says.

We three walk toward the rest of the gang, who are standing with two other very distinguished couples.

"Olivia, Thomas I would like you to meet some very dear old friends," Margarite announces.

"The *dear* part is quite flattering but I don't feel *old.* Geoffrey and my long suffering wife, Anne." He extends his hand, which I shake. Olivia tries to do the same but gets a kiss on the fingers instead. His accent is terribly British.

"Geoffrey is the former chief of information for MI 6. We've worked together for a long time." Hans inserts.

"Hans, if you measure in decades instead of years, it has only been about five." Anne McDonald has a sense of humor totally compatible with our hosts.

"And my former wife's brother, Jacque Miello and his beautiful bride Maria." Pierre holds both of their hands.

"Bon jour." Instead of a hand shake, we each get a double kiss on the cheeks from the Miellos. Pierre only kisses Olivia. Then gives me a French shrug.

"May I ask a sensitive question?" Detective Nederfield is very careful with her selection of words.

"But of course," Pierre answers.

"How is it you have stayed so close to your former wife's family, as well as your own?"

"I am a widower and we have always been friends." Another shrug.

"Excusez-moi. Pierre's wife Suzanne was the most wonderful woman. She worked very closely with us all, but cancer took her far too early," Maria Miello explains.

I am curious but afraid to ask what kind of work everyone did.

"Enough! It has been a long day and we have many fishing lines in the water. Tomorrow is another day. In celebration of Jacque's retirement as director general of the Sûretè, Stanford has made his world famous coq au vin. Franco has selected a very nice Pinot Noir from New Zealand in recognition of Anne's place of birth."

"We have one more guest to introduce. Thomas, do the honors," Margarite commands-nicely. I am at a loss until I see Young Don Montgomery walking over from the showers, wearing his team shirt, as promised.

"I want you all to meet Donald Montgomery, about whom I just wrote an article, describing him as the new driver to watch." I hope I didn't embarrass the kid but this group is very low key, even if it now includes the former heads of two of the world's largest spy organizations.

"May I get you some liquid refreshment?" Franco asks.

"If it's not much of a bother, may I have a Dr. Pepper?" Olivia and I can hardly contain ourselves. We get a severe look from Margarite.

"Absolument. We have some on ice." This time she gives us a smile and a wink and Franco rushes off, returning with a can in a Bentley koozie.

"Merci!" The young race driver responds.

Cecil approaches Don and puts his arm of the young man's shoulder. "When do you go out tomorrow?"

"We have a 40 lap qualifying race at 11:00."

"Do you need any help with the car?" Cecil asks.

"I would like to have another pair of eyes go over my pre-race check list with me. Uncle Cosmo used to do it. I don't want anything to go wrong. I think the car is dialed in pretty well but I feel a little loose going into turn 1."

"Only there?" Frederick joins the conversation.

"Yes. I feel the car lifting a little."

"We need to adjust the track bar. Just a little. I will help you tomorrow morning. We do not race until 1 o'clock. Cecil, don't you agree that we are ready to go?"

"A splash of petro, check tire pressure and oil level and we are, as they say, good to go."

"We have been ordered that we cannot discuss business tonight, but is it okay if Geoffrey, Anne, Jacques and Maria join us for the briefing tomorrow?" Hans seems to be directed the question to Olivia and me, but this is their investigation.

"Wow! It would be an honor." I notice that the McDonalds and the Miellos ever so slightly nod their heads. Why do I think this team has been assembled many times before?

"Hans, we have asked Sheriffs McCarthy and Wetherford to join us," Olivia adds.

"One meal at a time. That is all I can think about and we must eat this feast before it gets cold." Stanford hustles off to add the final touches to what smells like heaven in a pot.

"We have set up a dining table next to Cecil's motor coach and we have been ordered to relocate ourselves forthwith," Charles announces gesturing like he is ringing the dinner bell.

We all oblige. How does Stanford do it? Maybe in a former life he was the chef at The Clove Club in London or Septime in Paris or Le Bernardin in New York. Why in another life? These folks seem to have done everything in this life.

CHAPTER FORTY-THREE

Dinner was fantastic, wine was incomparable, conversation was stimulating, but now it is time to take our leave. Tomorrow morning will arrive early.

"Signorina Olivia," Franco shouts as we begin to walk back to Nellie Belle. "Signore Thomas. Un momento. I almost forgot. This is a special port we found many years ago and wanted to serve it tonight, but mio Dio, I forgot." He hands us each in a miniature wine glass, emblazoned with the letter B. The dark red liquid is ambrosia. I have never been a real fan of port but that's probably because I have only tasted the cheap stuff. Not so with the Bentley Seven-plus one.

"Franco, thank you for tracking us down. The port is simply magnificent," Olivia purrs. She kisses Franco on the cheek. I may have to resuscitate the Italian sommelier.

"Tomorrow at eight and don't be late," Franco chuckles at the rhyme. "Quiche waits for no one. Ciao."

"That was a real treat," I say.

"Thomas is your cell vibrating or is your stomach making a strange noise?"

"Unless it's Josh, I am not expecting any calls," I reply. I seldom give out my cell number. First, there is really no need to get a hold of me other than email and secondly, I hate to be bothered. "Ballard, here," I answer. The caller ID says the phone is a local number, but I don't recognize it. "Wait a second while I put you on speaker," I say. "You sound upset, Don."

Olivia nods in recognition.

"He was at my trailer when I got back from dinner."

"Who?"

"The man in the picture, Jung Kim."

"Don, this is Olivia. Can you meet us at our trailer in five minutes?"

"Sure."

"We can talk in private. Take a couple of deep breaths. You aren't hurt are you?" Detective Nederfield is obviously very concerned. I am confused.

"No. It was nothing like that at all. I'll be right over." We end the call.

"Why do I have a sense that the dots are getting further apart rather than closer together?" I ask no one in particular, but since I am next to the lovely Detective Nederfield, maybe she can shed some light on this.

"Stop thinking, Thomas, it put wrinkles on your brow. We will know the answer momentarily."

Damn, I hate it when she's right, which is like all the time. I pick up the pace.

We arrive at Nellie Belle about ten seconds before Don Montgomery comes jogging around the side.

"Thanks for seeing me." Cosmo Costello may have been a hood, but he taught the kid to be polite.

"Come on in," Olivia says.

I turn on the few low wattage lights we have so that at least we can see.

"Can I get you something to drink?" I ask.

"Do you have Dr. Pepper?" The reply brings a smile to my face. Same with Olivia.

"What would you like to drink, my dear?" I know I sound a bit informal, but I want to put young Montgomery at ease.

"Thomas, I'll split a Dr. Pepper with you. Plenty of ice."

"Coming up."

After serving the drinks, we settle in. The Airstream may be old, but it was built in the days when comfort was king.

"Donald, we have plenty of time, so tell us what happened . . . slowly," Detective Nederfield begins.

"After dinner, which was great . . . Uncle Cosmo loved good food and this was a spectacular meal. Oh. When I got back to my trailer Mr. Kim and that other fellow were waiting for me. Mr. Kim initially asked to speak to my uncle, which I thought strange. He said that he had called my uncle about a week ago, after they had talked at Fruitfield, and he apologized for being a bit too assertive. That was the word he used. His accent was completely American. He said that they had agreed to meet at Daytona. Mr. Kim also said he had all the paperwork Uncle Cosmo requested and he hoped they could reach an agreement before qualifying tomorrow. I was a little confused, but I decided to play along and replied that he might arrive late tonight but certainly by noon tomorrow for qualifying. Mr. Kim asked if he could leave some papers for my uncle to review and that he would return around ten . . . if that was satisfactory to me. I said that ten was fine. I made a point of shaking hands with both men, so I could get a good look at the face of the other man. Here's everything he gave me. I only glanced at it. I was spooked. I may be young and naïve, but I don't think that Mr. Kim has any idea my uncle is dead."

"Don could you sit with Charles and do a sketch of the other man?"

"Yes. I got a good look at him."

Before I could retrieve my phone from my jacket pocket, Detective Nederfield was dialing. "Hans, this is Olivia. May I put you on speaker?"

He obviously agreed since he immediately asked, "Is everything alright?"

"Yes, but something has come up and despite Margarite's rule on discussing business, this cannot wait. May Olivia, Don Montgomery and I come over right now? We will need Charles' services as well."

"I'm intrigued. Please come by."

"Thanks. We will be there in ten minutes." I nod to Olivia who returns the phone to her oversized handbag.

"I don't want to make this too long. You've have a qualifying session and Frederick wants to tweak your suspension."

"That's only part of it. Kim Tires has offered me a deal to use their tires. The papers include technical stuff, performance charts, temperature charts . . . a complete engineering analysis. I bet my uncle demanded that Kim secure permission from NASCAR to use the tires before he would talk about sponsorship . . . and he got it."

"Let's get back to headquarters. I am seriously overloading," I say.

CHAPTER FORTY-FOUR

During our journey to the Bentley Seven's RV, our hosts have transformed their living quarters back into a war room complete with flat screen monitors. Joining the team, which now includes Cecil, are both the McDonalds and the Miellos. Talk about the *A Team.*

"Welcome," Margarite says as we enter. "I know you would never call us if it was not of significant urgency. Please be seated. We all know each other so let us begin."

"May I?" I want to direct attention to three things: the visit with Kim; the papers he left and the identity of the heretofore unknown man. "I think we should start with the fact that Jung Kim dropped in on Donald this evening."

"Interesting," Hans mutters.

"Equally interesting may be what is in the papers he left ostensibly for Cosmos Costello to review. There seems to be both a technical component to the documents which I would like Frederick to review and both a letter from NASCAR and a proposed sponsorship agreement which I think Cecil should examine. Lastly, because Donald is a resourceful young man, he was able to get a good look at the fellow who accompanies Kim. Maybe he and Charles could create an image that might help identify this mystery man."

"I have connected my drawing board to the monitors so that we can see the image together. Mr. Montgomery, please describe the man's head shape: round; elongated, narrow at the top or bottom?" This procedure goes on for about ten minutes until we all are looking at a picture of the ordinary looking man always lurking in the background. He does look rather unremarkable except for a small scar on the bridge of his nose, his rather full lips, his eyes being just a bit far apart and several other very minor features that one would not observe unless prompted by an expert like Charles.

"Superficially he looks rather like anyone else. We always tried to hire agents with bland features so that they could not be identified. Charles, you are as brilliant as always," Geoffrey McDonald observes.

"From you, Sir Geoffrey, that is a most flattering compliment," Charles replies.

The people in the inner circle of the Bentley Seven are seriously impressive.

"Charles, please send me the image and I will forward it to our resources," Hans says.

"Please leave it on the screen as well. There is something very familiar about that chap. Mr. Montgomery, how tall would you estimate the stranger is?" Sir Geoffrey is going somewhere.

"When I shook hands with him, I looked him directly in the eye, as Uncle Cosmo always told me to do. He was standing up straight. I think I took him off guard by extending my hand to him. We looked at each other on the level, so I would say we were the same height; six foot. He was not terribly athletic looking, but he was not fat. In fact, he wasn't thin either."

"What do you mean he wasn't athletic looking?" Maria Miello asks.

"He didn't have a thick neck or broad shoulders. It's hard to describe," Don replied.

"Sir Geoffrey is correct, the man is too normal," Jacques Miello adds.

"Charles, does the face have any racial or ethnic indicators?" I ask.

"If I had to guess, I would say European ancestry. Probably from the Mediterranean. Spain. Hidalgo. His family has been in the Americas for many generations, but did not intermingle. California or Baja."

I am tempted to ask if he could provide an address or at least a zip code, but I do not think this is a time for levity. So much for Ancestry.com.

"I have found something rather interesting," Cecil inserts. "The letter included in the documents Mr. Montgomery gave me is indeed from NASCAR and grants our friend permission to use Kim racing tires in qualifying here at Daytona, but not qualifying for the Trophy series.

"That's not a problem because Don's car is not in the Trophy series," I insert.

"The letter goes on to say that the tires must be removed, impounded and examined by the chief tech inspector who will determine if the tires are safe after each session. He is not to offer any opinion regarding the performance of the tire, only whether they showed any signs of being unsafe. If the car is in an accident and a tire replacement is necessitated, the damaged tire will be examined by the NASCAR safety committee in North Carolina as soon as possible, but the car will not be permitted to compete on Kim tires until the results are verified."

"Cecil, I am curious. I had understood that Juan Carlos Cidado was racing and winning using Kim tires," I ask.

"The letter applies to Daytona only and specifically says that cars may be shod with Kim tires for events on tracks that are under a mile in length and for races no longer than 50 miles," Cecil continues. "What is equally interesting is that Kim Tires offered Mr. Montgomery's uncle a sponsorship deal worth $20,000 for Daytona provided he compete in qualifying as well as the feature, plus as many sets of tires as are required and technical help."

"I'll bet that is why Kim was trying to get the Goodyear guy to mount his tires," Olivia adds.

"Do you think there is any connection between the vandalism to Juan Carolos' tire and Kim?" I ask.

"As I understand the rules," Cecil begins, "NASCAR has an exclusive arrangement with Goodyear for the Trophy series. So there is no need to damage Juan Carolos' tire, which was a Goodyear. The team would put on another set of the same. Kim Tires are not an alternative."

"This may be far-fetched, but could it have been some kind of warning to Juan Carlos regarding Kim tires?" Olivia asks.

"Damaging Juan Carlos at the Trophy level actually hurts Kim Tires. If a successful tier one driver elects to use Kim Tires when he is driving tier two races, it puts more pressure on NASCAR to relax its rules and raises brand recognition," Cecil correctly deduces.

"Let's return to the contract with Team Montgomery and Kim Tires." I am concerned we are drifting and we have precious little time to leave the main line of inquiry.

"Perfectly straight forward and there is a check for ten thousand dollars attached noting, *first installment.*"

Sounds like a dream come true for the young driver. What's wrong?

"Don, you mentioned that Jung Kim had apologized to your uncle," Detective Nederfield inserts.

"That's what he said. He felt he had gotten a little intense in putting forth his proposal to Uncle Cosmo. I was a distance away from them and did not hear anything. They both use their hands a lot when talking so maybe what I thought was anger was really the two of them engaging in business discussions."

"Did your uncle ever mention a potential sponsorship deal?" Olivia asks.

"He did and he didn't. He was always coy and believed that if you talked about a deal before it was done, you jinxed it. He seemed very pleased with the way certain discussions were going, but I didn't know what he was referring to. In our family, one didn't ask questions."

"So maybe Kim and your uncle were negotiating not fighting." My question is a bit rhetorical.

Before Don gets a chance to answer, Frederick says, "The technical information included in the material for your uncle is quite impressive. Kim Tires seems to have produced a very high quality performance tire with major implications. Traction and wear have historically been related; the more traction, the faster the tires wear probably because of the softer compound and thus tires need to be changed more often. Kim seems to have engineered a product with superb traction and excellent wear. Mr. Montgomery, I suggest you accept the offer and race tomorrow on Kim tires. I will make a few changes to your setup to reflect the new technical specifications."

"We seem to have been making a case to eliminate Jung Kim as a suspect," I suggest.

"I have been thinking about Olivia's comment that the vandalized tire may be a warning. Maybe it is, but has nothing to do with Juan Carlos or Kim, but Henry Fuller, about whom many questions remain unanswered." I want to know more about the last twenty years of dear Henry's life.

"The hour is late. We have sent out Charles' sketch. Sir Geoffrey and Jacque have added their resources to our investigation. The importation and distribution of drugs has worldwide implications. Cecil you are scheduled to race at 1:00, yes?" Cecil nods to Hans. "And Donald, you race at noon, correct?" The young driver nods. "And Frederick, will you be able to prepare both cars within the allotted time?" Frederick nods. "Pierre and Franco, can you help Frederick with the cars?" They both nod. "Charles, please walk around the entire paddock area and photograph anything that may be interesting. People love their photographs taken so a subtle question or two might be in order." Charles signals by giving a *thumbs up*. "Stanford, can you manage alone?" He nods.

"Maria and I can help Stanford. Working with a great chef is an honor," Anne McDonald offers.

"Jacques, Geoffrey, Margarite and I will gather what information we can. What time are you meeting Mr. Kim?" Hans asks Don Montgomery.

"At 10:00, sir."

"Cecil, can you be at Mr. Montgomery's trailer a few minutes before the appointment just in case any last minute legal issues arise?" Cecil nods.

Hans has made everything clear, except that Olivia and I don't have assignments. I raise my hand.

"Thomas, you and Olivia are in charge of bringing both Sheriff McCarthy and Sheriff Wetherford up to speed. I suggest that you brief them here at 8 o'clock as originally planned in case they have a question for any of us. Thereafter, I suggest that you track down Henry Fuller. Hopefully with the data we collect overnight, we will be able to place him into the matrix or exclude him. As you are undoubtedly thinking, he is what we call a wild card."

How does Hans know that is what I am thinking? Don't ask."

CHAPTER FORTY-FIVE

I am not looking forward to briefing Josh and Mike in large part because I am not sure we have made a lot of progress except one more murder and one *accident* which could have resulted in serious injury to Juan Carlos. I am still trying to connect his family with both the Kim family and with Henry Fuller . . . and maybe the murders of the couriers and Cosmo.

"Good night darling," I whisper.

"Try to get some sleep, Thomas. I think that tomorrow will be a rather full day." Olivia slides over and gives me a hug and kiss. It certainly makes me feel reassured that everything will be alright. "I am setting the alarm for 6:00 so that we can get in a little track time."

"Track time?"

"We need to run off all the fantastic food we've been eating. Also it clears the brain. Two laps around the track. We can run the apron."

"Actually, that sounds like a good idea. It's just another reason why I love you." This time I slide over and give Olivia a hug and kiss.

Although the alarm goes off entirely too early, after two rather brisk laps on the iconic track, a hot shower, shave and some fresh clothes, I feel like a new man, although I still like the old one. "I'll make some coffee," I announce to a closed door, behind which Olivia is making herself even more beautiful.

Our domestic bliss is interrupted by a knock on the door of the Airstream, immediately followed by Sheriff Josh McCarthy and Sheriff Mike Wetherford, the former holding a bag of donuts and the latter four cups of steaming coffee.

"Don't you wait until some says *enter* or *come in* before you open the door?" I ask.

"We've been walking into each other's houses for over four decades," Josh answers.

"Yeah, but have you forgotten that Detective Nederfield might not be ready to receive company." I sound a little righteously indignant.

The door opens and Olivia enters. She always reminds me of Lauren Bacall but prettier and taller. "Good morning gentlemen." Her voice is like silk. Both Josh and Mike have their respective mouths open but nothing is coming out.

"Es-he-thio-se," Sheriff Wetherford stammers.

Olivia, Josh and I stare.

"Sorry. It means totally awesome in my native tongue. Well, it means pretty or beautiful in Muscogee."

"Thank you Sheriff . . . and I would love a cup of coffee."

Our senior law enforcement officials snap out of their trance. I've seen it before and if they think Detective Nederfield wearing chinos and a Hudson team shirt is special, you should see her in a strapless black cocktail dress with pearls and three inch heels.

Three sips later, there is another knock on the door. "Buongiorrno. Margarite wants you to come right away. Not only has Stanford made a special breakfast, but Hans and

Cecil have been downloading data for over an hour already. Come. I have the golf cart. Sheriff McCarthy, please sit up front and Sheriff Wetherford, please sit in the way back."

"Way back?"

"Sì. It is the seat that faces backwards . . . the way back. I want to balance the weight." Franco is chipper this morning. I bet he has had more than a few sips of java already.

Stanford has set up a buffet table outside *headquarters.* Not only are the heretofore mentioned quiches on display, but a fruit salad of every imaginable melon and berry serves as the centerpiece. The more mundane items such as fresh biscuits with butter and jam, grits (this is the South remember), juices, coffee and tea are scattered about. Needless to say, there are neither paper plates nor plastic spoons. In addition to the regulars, the McDonald's and Miello's have risen early to join us.

"Hinclus hompusche o-hom-pee-tah," Sheriff Wetherford sputters.

"Alaha we-waw?" Frederick asks, handing Sheriff Mike a glass of orange juice.

"You speak our language?"

"And he speaks many, many more. We haven't met. My name is Geoffrey McDonald and this is my wife, Anne."

"My Seminole is a bit rusty, please translate." I ask.

"Our guest complimented the breakfast table and I offered him an orange juice," Frederick says, grinning from ear to ear.

"Okay, Josh, what's up?"

"Don't ask," Orange County Sheriff McCarthy replies.

"Gentlemen, I want you to meet our other guests . . . Jacque and Maria Miello." Margarite reasserts control.

"Director General Miello?" Josh asks.

"Oui, but now retired," Jacque replies.

"Mike, Monsieur Miello is the former head of the *Sûretè.*"

"I am investigating a murder by blunt instrument with one of the world's most famous policeman?" I think Mike better drink his orange juice.

"All murders are important and we may have solved yours already," Hans says. "The murder weapon has only two sets of fingerprints; those of the deceased and those of Stephen Henderson, a member of the pit crew on Team Henry Fuller. We are exploring a motive as well."

I guess I am relieved that one murder has been solved, but it seems the most remote from our investigation, maybe. If Hans can pin down a motive, the means and the opportunity, it's a slam dunk. Why am I so unsure?

"Should we arrest him on at least suspicion of murder?" Sheriff Wetherford asks.

"When your deputies went to his motel room last night to get his fingerprints, one of the other members of the pit crew said that he left rather abruptly," Hans replied.

"How do you know?" Sheriff Mike is getting very nervous. He looks at Josh who shakes his head. "Shall I issue an arrest warrant and put out an APB?"

"He is presently on I-77 just south of Columbia, South Carolina and is being followed by two unmarked cars."

"But he is a murder suspect here in my county."

"He may be a part of something larger. Once I was made aware late last night that he left the state of Florida, I was able to get a Federal stop and hold order, but we need to see where he goes. If his actions were somewhat spontaneous as a result of a confrontation with Harvey Silver over personal issues, then he will be returned immediately. If he is a pawn in a larger game, he will be shadowed until his role is ascertained."

"Sheriff Wetherford, please have faith in our decisions. All will be as it should." Margarite walks over next to Hans. So do Olivia and I.

"Mike, throw away everything you ever learned about law enforcement and watch these folks. Please trust them . . . and me." Josh speaks in whispered tones.

"As Chief of Information at MI 6, I was trained to rely on hard data until I started working with Hans and his team. They have never, and I mean never failed."

"Sir Geoffrey, please do not place any more onto the Sheriff's shoulders. Let's eat and review what our fish net has brought in." Hans walks over to the visibly shaking Sheriff Wetherford and says, *"Esse-ka-phutena-la.* Peace be with you."

"Cha. And with you." The two men walk toward the breakfast table.

CHAPTER FORTY-SIX

It seems like the calm before the storm. Stanford's offerings were wonderful as usual. The conversation was especially enjoyable when Sir Geoffrey started to tell us stories about acting as a consultant for several of the James Bond movies, especially when the Aston Martin ran out of gas not once but twice during production. It seems that the gas gauge had been wired incorrectly so that as gas was used needle went toward full not empty. Lucas, the Prince of Darkness, strikes again.

"It is time to review the material received overnight. Jacque's sources were the first to identify the man who is always with Jung Kim. His name is Bernardo Lopez, Marcel Piña, Franz Santiago, Richard French . . . shall I continue? Nevertheless he is the same man and is a chief inspector at Interpol, assigned to Central America, Mexico and Southern California as a facilitator to help coordinate drug enforcement. His birth name is Joaquin Luis de la Herrera. He was born in San Diego, attended University of Southern California where he majored in criminal justice, joined the California State Police and was traded to Interpol three years later."

"Traded? Like baseball?" Sheriff Mike asks.

"Almost. There are hundreds of interagency transfers each year throughout the world."

"That is how MI 6 first met Hans and the group. They were loaned to us for a rather sticky investigation," Sir Geoffrey inserts.

"Oui. Same with the Sûretè," Inspector General Miello adds.

"In any event, de la Herrera is a really important part of the war on the movement of illegal drugs through South and Central America to the United States," Hans finishes.

"What is the connection with Kim?" I ask.

"There are several answers to your question, Thomas. Please be patient," Margarite says. "My sources seem to think that Jung Kim is not the bad boy of the Kim family, but rather a highly placed member of the Korean intelligence community. He has assumed the persona of a tire salesman as a so-called *cover*. Drug trafficking in Asia is as severe as the rest of the world. Transportation is the critical feature. About fifteen years ago, a large shipment of cocaine was intercepted quite by accident. The dogs had not detected the presence of the substance, but the cargo had shifted somewhat in transit and a package of the drug literally fell out of the container. The cargo in the container was tires which when new give off an odor than blocks the ability of the dogs to sniff out the cocaine. The drug dealers have been using this technique for some time. Law enforcement did not want to reveal that it had figured out the methodology, so they began to monitor tire deliveries worldwide, intercepting deliveries at random so that it did not appear that tire shipments were being targeted. Jung Kim convinced his father and brother to purchase a tire company."

"Excuse me Margarite, but why would the Kim's want to buy a tire company?" Detective Nederfield asks the question we have been wondering for several days.

"To penetrate the distribution network and then disrupt it," Hans answers.

"It was a very ambitious undertaking. Korean intelligence correctly concluded that the fewer people who knew about Kim's plan, the better. So he began to develop a tire that would give him credibility, leverage and ultimately dominance. Money was no object. Rather than enter the United States market directly, Jung Kim decided to concentrate on South America where so much of the product was produced. He recruited his brother-in-law, Juan Carolos' father, as the distributor. Georgio owned a large ranch, but was having money problems. Cecil, I am running out of breath. Please continue."

"Here, a glass of Perrier for your thirst," the ubiquitous Franco offers.

"Merci."

"Prego."

"Georgio Cidado was a hard worker, and with the economic backing of Kim Enterprises, he was able to impact the sales of tires in Argentina, Uruguay and Brazil and deeply penetrate into the market with both a less expensive and a better quality product. Enter Henry Fuller." Cecil pauses for us to absorb what is being said.

"Now it's getting interesting," I quip. "By the way, does anyone know where he is?"

"According to the GPS we placed on his car, he is on I 95 about fifty miles north of Fort Lauderdale, with a one way ticket to Cartagena." Frederick nods.

"I'm sorry to sound like a cop, but I am. How do we prevent Mr. Fuller from fleeing the jurisdiction?" Josh doesn't want to lose a witness like Sheriff Mike almost did.

"The wonders of modern science. His name is now on a no fly list and when he presents his passport to TSA, he will be told that there is a problem. Before the problem is resolved, several agents will accompany Mr. Fuller to a convenient location." Charles is keeping us on the edge of our seats.

"Which is?" I can't resist asking.

"Why Chez Bentley, of course," Pierre chimes.

"Here?" Sheriff Wetherford is almost squeaking.

Hans says, "It is the least we can do. We took away one suspect from you but we are exchanging him for another, Mr. Fuller."

"When is he expected to arrive? The helicopter to transport him here is being readied as we speak. Correct Sir Geoffrey?"

"The RAF stands ready to assist. It has received clearance and will take off shortly. Between flight time, tarmac time and paperwork, Mr. Fuller can be expected just about the time Cecil finishes his race."

Josh is shrugging. Mike is quivering. Olivia and I simply take all this in as *business as usual.*

"Cecil, you said, *Enter Henry Fuller,* what did you mean?"

"Thomas, I think the Henry Fuller saga will be told when the fellow gets here. I want him to hear it in person since it will make questioning more poignant."

"Since Olivia and I were to seek out Henry Fuller, I presume we are free to wander around. I might even find something to write about."

At that instant Sheriff McCarthy's cell phone starts to ring. It sounds like a police siren. He actually looks at the caller ID before, rather than after, answering. "Hi Helen. What's up? No shit! Oops. Sorry. I'll be there within an hour." Josh returns his phone to his pocket. "Since it doesn't look like the fireworks will begin before two, after Cecil's race, I have to scoot back to the office. Just another murder. Same old, same old."

"Do we know the victim?" Olivia asks.

"Damien LeValle, Jr. Pimp, small time drug dealer, nothing special."

"Does he drive a fuchsia older model Cadillac?" Olivia continues.

"That's the guy. I hate to speak badly of the dead, but I am glad he is off the street. I'll be back in a couple of hours. Stanford, the quiche was out of this world. Do you happen to have a Dr. Pepper for the road?"

"Better be the only one you drink today. I am going to call Helen." I can be so mean, but it's for his own good. Just like your mother always said.

"I had better head back to the office for a little paperwork as well," Sheriff Wetherford sighs. "But I'll be back."

Josh puts his burly arm over Mike's shoulder, "Let's go Tonto."

"Okay Kemo Sabe."

"Gentlemen, that's not politically correct." I can't tell if Olivia is serious or kidding.

"She's right," Mike says. "Next time you are Tonto, I'll be Kemo Sabe." The two sheriffs start laughing.

CHAPTER FORTY-SEVEN

"Gentlemen," Frederick says. "We need to high step it over to young Montgomery's rig, make adjustments, give the car a visual and return post haste to the Hudson." Cecil, Pierre, Franco and Frederick rise in perfect synchronization and exit, leaving the Leiters, the McDonalds, the Miellos, Olivia and me. Stanford is already bustling around the kitchen.

Annoyingly my cell phone starts to vibrate. The caller ID says *out of area,* whatever that means. "Ballard here." I am a bit abrupt. "Let me put you on speaker. Olivia is here and she is trained in evasive driving." I shrug in response to a glare from Detective Nederfield.

"Thomas, I am in big trouble." Henry Fuller's voice cries over the speaker. Margarite, Hans, Sir Geoffrey and Jacque move closer.

"Slow down Henry and start from the beginning."

"I need to tell you in person. You are the only one I can trust."

"Okay, do you want to meet me at my trailer in ten minutes?" Several eye brows are raised. Hans moves to his computer and projects Fuller's GPS location-a little north of Delray Beach traveling south on I-95 at 79 miles per hour.

"I can't. I'm not at the track."

"But you have two cars qualifying this afternoon and the Chief Steward is looking for you because of the tire damage." I decide to fib a little and string him along a little.

"I'm not at the track. I'm driving to Fort Lauderdale and I am being followed." Everyone in the room looks at one another. Hans enters a few commands into the computer and two red flashing dots appear on the monitor behind the blue dot which I assume is Fuller's car.

"Describe the car?"

"It is a pearl white late model Cadillac Escalade and he has been behind since I left Daytona."

Hans shakes his head and furiously writes the following on a piece of paper which Sir Geoffrey hands me. *One of our surveillance cars is a new silver Mustang and the other is a black 4 door Infiniti.*

We all nod. "Henry, this is Olivia. I want you to exit onto Route 806 and re-enter I-95 heading north. Use your blinker, turn on your headlights and do not exceed 72 miles per hour. Call Thomas when you reach the intersection of I-4 and I-95 south of Daytona. Understood?"

"Yes. What if he still follows me?"

"If he is following you now, we assume he will continue to follow you. Do not try to shake him. We will set everything up at our end."

"Okay. I see the sign for Route 806."

Olivia returns the phone to me. "Henry, it should take you around three hours. If you need gas get off the interstate and go directly to the nearest station. There are signs at each exit which will tell you what services are available and how close they are to the exit. Use the closest one and don't leave I-95 until the little red gas light goes on. Concentrate on the road ahead. Don't worry what is behind you. Don't forget to call me."

"Thanks Thomas. You are a life saver." I push the *END* button.

"Do you think it is too early for a stiff drink?" I ask only half kiddingly.

"Sir Geoffrey, I think the RAF should stand down, but still be at alert status," Hans says. "I am going to have one car follow Fuller and the other the Cadillac . . . just in case." He types something into his computer. We all look at the screen and see the blue dot heading north. One of the red dots follows. A minute later, the second red dot appears somewhat in arrears but traveling at over 80. "I assume the Cadillac decided to follow Mr. Fuller and our agent had to play catch up."

"We have had a rather exciting morning," Sir Geoffrey says. "Although I prefer champagne, a strong cup of tea is quite in order."

"Wonderful idea," I add.

I am convinced Stanford has eyes and ears everywhere. He suddenly appears with a tray upon which he has placed eight steaming mugs. "Margarite, Maria and Jacque, I have blended your coffee just the way you like it. Olivia, Hans and Charles your coffee is a little less bitter and two cups of tea; for you Sir Geoffrey and you Thomas. Crème, sugar, honey and lemon are on the tray. I threw in a few croissants which should be ready in about five minutes. Anything else?"

"Join us, dear friend," Margarite says.

"Thank you but I have two assistants awaiting orders from the chef . . . *moi.*"

"Hans, I think we should have Mr. Henderson returned," I suggest.

"I agree. Now that the Fuller caravan is heading back, it might be best if everyone is present. Sir Geoffrey, could we impose upon your helicopter unit and divert them to the Charlotte-Douglas Airport?"

"Hans, should I instruct the pilot to use the Air Center Terminal? He has military clearance."

"Excellent. I'll tell the agents to pick him up in Belmont, which is about twenty miles west of the airport and take him to the air center."

"How do you know he is going to Belmont, North Carolina?" I think my question is logical.

"That's where Harvey Silver's now widow lives. Apparently they have been having a rather serious affair."

"Makes sense." I could really use another cup of tea.

"I think that we need to think about integrating Jung Kim and Joaquin Luis de la Herrera into our investigation." Olivia is reading my mind, such as it is.

"We must also consider Juan Carlos Cidado," I offer.

"Our timetable is quite tight," Sir Geoffrey observes. "The ten o'clock meeting with Kim is being handled. His race is at noon. Cecil's race is immediately after. Henry Fuller should arrive by 1:30. Sheriff McCarthy is returning about the same time, as is Sheriff Wetherford. Mr. Henderson should be here about 2:00, depending on logistics. Am I forgetting anything or anyone?"

"Thomas after you have fortified yourself with another cup of tea and a couple of Stanford's croissants, I think a chat with Juan Carlos is the next order of business. Margarite, Sir Geoffrey, Jacque and I still need a little computer time and we only have a little more than an hour." Hans is interrupted by a beeping sound on his phone signaling receipt of a text message. "The white Cadillac Escalade following Mr.

Fuller was stolen from the Miami International Airport from a rental agency on Wednesday. It wasn't reported until this morning since our clever crooks swapped plates with another car so the Cadillac appeared in inventory."

"Thomas and I will check in at the Fuller garage and track down Juan Carlos. But first I think we should decide how to bring Mr. Kim and Mr. de la Herrera into the investigation. More than likely, they can add information to our efforts."

"I have found that the straightforward approach is always the best," Sir Geoffrey offers.

"Why don't we simply walk up to them, address them by name, show them our badges and invite them to meet here at 2?" I hope I don't sound too glib, but it is straightforward.

"Capital idea. I suggest you go now. We know they are with young Montgomery and Cecil, Frederick, Pierre and Franco are with him.

Stanford bustles out of the kitchen area with a napkin which is warm to the touch. "This should tide you over until lunch, which will be a bit late today because of Cecil's race."

"You are too kind," I lamely reply.

"I know," Stanford answers with a wink.

CHAPTER FORTY-EIGHT

We elect to visit team Fuller first to see if the deputies on duty need anything. As we approach the garage that houses the wrecked car of Juan Carlos, we run into none other than Juan Carlos, sporting a lime green cast on his left arm.

"Que pasó?" Olivia asks.

"Do you like the color? I had a choice."

Detective Nederfield says, "Juan Carlos, please do not act as if this is a joke."

"Lo siento. I am sorry. Last night my arm started to hurt very badly, so I called Jung Kim. He is my uncle, más o menos. He looked at my arm and pointed out a very thin bruise and took me to the hospital. The x-ray showed a fracture, not serious, but certainly needing a cast. They gave me something for the pain and all I remember is my tío suggesting to the doctor that because of the accident, it might be best if I stay the night under observation. One does not argue with Jung Kim and I was moved to a room. He picked me up at 8:00 and decided I needed a good breakfast. We ate at a very nice restaurant. I was starving. He said he had a meeting and returned me here about 10 minutes ago. I was looking for Mr. Fuller to tell him the bad news. No racing for three

weeks. I might go back to Buenos Aires. Have you seen Mr. Fuller and why are there policemen here?"

I am exhausted just listening to Juan Carlos, although to his credit, he did tell us the whole story.

"Someone from the health department found very high levels of toxic fumes and the garage area had to be evacuated. That is why the yellow tape says *CAUTION—GAS LEAK.* The sheriff's office doesn't want anyone getting too close until the fumes have been cleared." I think Olivia did a great job of improvisation.

"When is that?"

"I talked with Mr. Fuller and everything should be back to normal by 3 o'clock," I add.

"We would not have been able to race anyway, si?"

"The crew is not expected back until then. We need to interview some people for an article about vintage stock car racing so we must go. But maybe you can meet us for a drink later?

"Gracias. I would like that."

"And Juan Carlos . . . you look good in green," Olivia says. The kid is all smiles. He may be a spoiled brat sometimes, but basically, he's only 19 years old.

"Let's hustle over to Team Montgomery. No time like the present to be straightforward, as Sir Geoffrey pointed out." I hook my arm into Olivia's and together we walk and skip.

On a race weekend of this magnitude, there is precious little space that is not filled with something-tractor-trailers, vendors, spectators and nemesis of everyone trying to navigate through the maze-golf carts, scooters and other devices that look like they just came from a grocery store. The drivers are not aware of the speed at which they travel, the amount of space the vehicle occupies and the basic courtesies that should be exercised in a huge crowd. I have been tempted to take an old umbrella and jam it into the spokes of their wheels. By the time I have been considering all this, we arrive at a veritable bee-hive of activity at Donald's garage, which is really an open shed in which about thirty other drivers are working on their cars. The difference is that there seems to be less chaos. Several men wearing Kim Tire uniforms are huddling with Frederick. Three sets of brand new racing tires are neatly stacked, ready for installation. Jung Kim is making notes on a clip board and the mysterious Mr. de la Herrera is making himself as inconspicuous as possible. Franco emerges from behind the race car with young Montgomery's driver's suit, which he is vigorously brushing with a wooden handled brush designed more for a tuxedo than a fire proof suit. The drivers, Cecil and Don, are looking at a map of the roval configurations and comparing observations.

Pierre, who is lying on a creeper, scoots out from under the car and says to Frederick, "I have checked the torque of every nut and bolt in the front end. Mademoiselle Olivia . . . welcome."

He leaps up from the creeper and is about to greet her on the French way- a kiss to each cheek, when Olivia hands Pierre a *handy wipe.*

"But of course," He laughs, wipes his hands and then eagerly accepts Olivia's cheek.

"Mr. Kim, may I have a word with you?" I ask. "And you too Mr. de la Herrera." Now that got their attention. Jung Kim approaches me somewhat hurriedly.

"What is the meaning of this?" His English is accent free.

I show him my badge. Olivia does the same. Sensing that we may need a little more law enforcement authority, Franco once again produces his card, which Kim stares at.

Mr. de la Herrera is as white as a ghost. Pierre, hands the Interpol representative a bottle of Pierre which he always keeps close. "May I introduce you a small portion of our tem?" Pierre begins

Jung Kim is clearly confused. What team? Car racing or something else?

"Let me quickly introduce myself. I am Cecil Llewellyn. I drive a vintage Hudson Hornet which we must get to post haste."

"Are you Cecil Llewellyn, the software designer?" Kim asks in adoration.

"The same."

"We use so many of your applications at Kim Enterprises."

"As long as the licensing fees are paid." Cecil laughs.

"And I am Frederick Voss."

"The Nobel laureate?"

"I was lucky."

I am totally blown away. I knew that the Bentley Seven, plus one, were awesome, but this is over the top.

"And I am Pierre Richard. My sister Margarite and brother-in-law are at our RV and wish to share with you some things of mutual interest at about 2, after Cecil's race."

"Pierre Richard of the Sûretè?"

Pierre shrugs in the Gallic way.

"And your sister is married to Hans Leiter?"

"Oui."

"These are only names we hear whispered." Joaquin Luis de la Herrera finally speaks.

"They are back at our mobile headquarters with Sir Geoffrey McDonald and Jacques Miello." I thought I might as well do some more name dropping, especially when we need Kim and de la Herrera to tell us everything they know.

"We must finish up here and then pay some attention to the Hudson," Cecil says. "We must keep up appearances."

Jung Kim says something in Korean to the two uniformed assistants who immediately start to install the Kim tires on the Team Montgomery race car. With pit crew precision, the car is lowered off the jack, spares tools and tires are placed in the trailer attached to the Kim golf cart and Donald is being helped into his driver's suit by Franco.

"If the car should have any problems, will there be a communications problem between drive and pit crew?" I ask, not too subtly.

"Absolutely not," Answers one the two members of the Kim crew. My brother and I both speak fluent English, as well as French and Mandarin, although I don't expect the latter will be necessary here in Florida." He smiles and gives us a *thumbs up.*

"Olivia and I are going to stay with Donald, but will join up with Team Hudson before the race."

"Don't bother coming back to the garage; just meet us in the paddock. I expect that unless one of Mr. Montgomery's colleagues makes a mess on the track, the sessions will be run very close together." Cecil starts to march off as the rest of the group piles into the Bentley Seven golf cart.

"Pre race jitters," Frederick whispers.

CHAPTER FORTY-NINE

Upon arriving at the Don's paddock, we watched his newly acquired pit crew work with amazing efficiency. Every inch of the car is visually inspected for what I believe is the tenth time today. Tire pressure and temperature is measured. A rather haughty steward approaches the Kim mechanics who asks condescendingly whether he will need an interpreter.

"For what?" I respond, while winking at the multi lingual mechanic.

"Who are you?" He demands.

"Crew Chief, Thomas Ballard," I curtly reply.

"The writer?"

"And crew chief."

"The car can't run on Kim tires unless it has been given a written waiver by NASCAR."

"I know."

"Do you have the letter?"

I move close to the Kim mechanic and whisper in his ear, "This guy is a jerk. I think he needs a bit of a lesson."

"Ah so," He replies in the worst Charlie Chan accent possible and hands me the aforesaid letter which I in turn, hand to the steward.

"Everything in order?" I ask.

"Seems to be. Carry on."

"Aye, aye sir!" The mechanic replies. We all break out in gales of laughter. Several other crews have watched this performance and have joined us in laughter at the expense of the steward. I hope he doesn't do something stupid. I think Detective Nederfield would enjoy cuffing the guy.

Olivia and I assume our seats in the elevated crew station; don our communication headsets and watch. Because only our crew is wearing the requisite fireproof protective suits and helmets, we cannot leave our seats until the checkered flag. They've got to change tires and fuel the car. All the other teams have four persons over the wall.

Donald is gridded third for the forty mile race. The gas/tire pit window is about 26–30 laps. The cars move onto the track behind the pace car. I kind of feel bad for Juan Carlos because this is where he should be racing. Well, not that bad. The start is rather routine, and the top cars line up in single file for the first couple of laps. Since this race is being run solely on the oval, old school stock car strategies are employed. Several cars try to dive in front of young Montgomery, but he handles those feints with ease. He seems very comfortable. Consistent and smooth. Suddenly, he drops toward the apron in an attempt to pass the second place car. His maneuver is met with an attempted block, but Donald has already anticipated the driver's move and easily passes on the high side and holds his momentum through the corner.

I tell him, "Well done." The head gear is remarkably easy to use, but I want him to concentrate on the race and not be distracted by me-the blabber mouth.

"The car handles so well. It is unbelievable." He replies.

At speeds over 150 miles per hour a second separating the cars translates into a distance of several car lengths. The two leading cars race like an invisible thread is connecting them. The teams are nearing the window and there hasn't been a yellow flag. This is above and beyond my pay grade.

"Bring him in now for gas only," Olivia says.

I give her a look.

The pit crew who also hears all the chatter on their head sets gives me a *thumbs up.*

"Donald, I want you to pit next time around for gas only provided the tires feel good."

"If it's possible, they are better than when we started the race."

"Do not panic and speed down pit lane. Everything is ready."

Montgomery's peels off the track and heads down pit lane at exactly one mile under the speed limit and pulls into the pit. One pit crew member starts to dump gas, while the other quickly runs around the car visually checking everything. He tears of the plastic windshield liner and waives his arm in a circular motion. Donald takes off. Elapsed time is 3.9 seconds. He rejoins the race in about 12th or 13th position. Because other cars are in the window, they pit seeking fuel and tires. The average pit stop for two tires and gas is over 9 seconds and four tires and gas will cost the driver 14–15 seconds. After all the other competitors have cycled through the their pit stops, Donald Montgomery is almost 5 seconds ahead of his nearest challenger and remains in the lead at the checker. Winning is good, winning at Daytona is great, even if it is a qualifying race. The Kim mechanics check tire pressure, temperature and wear as soon as Donald stops along pit lane and they enter the data into their cells phones.

The victor climbs out of his car and is greeted by confetti, scantily dressed young ladies and some non alcoholic beverage squirted from giant bottles. The ceremony is curtailed by the announcer.

"Will all vintage stock cars please come to the false grid?"

These events are choreographed as closely as possible and a yellow flag free race is a bonus.

"Thomas, look over there."

My eyes follow her pointing finger. Jung Kim is jogging, well fast walking, over to the smiling young driver. We wave and are about to leave when we are stopped by the otherwise taciturn de la Herrera. "We will meet you as you asked after this race at the yellow garages. Do you have a monitor onto which some images can be projected? They are on a flash drive."

"Yes. Everything needed is available."

"When Jung Kim told me of the program applications developed by Cecil Llewellyn being used by Kim Enterprises, I had no doubt that we can get access to everything we need. I look forward to meeting your esteemed colleagues." Joaquin Luis de la Herrera simply turns and walks away.

"Strange bird," I mutter.

"It takes all kinds. That's why some people buy purple cars," Detective Nederfield is being very erudite.

"Let's lend our support to the Purple Hornet," I suggest.

"I thought it was the Green Hornet."

"You are really wound up."

"You are talking to a winning crew chief."

"Co-crew chief," I remind the Detective.

"Jealous?"

I lean over and give her a kiss.

CHAPTER FIFTY

The fifty lap vintage race on the oval at Daytona is a hoot. The cars slide into the turns, the drivers barely saving the behemoths before crashing into the wall. I am definitely going to attend a couple more of these events. It would make a great article-*Those Daring Drivers of the Monsters of Steel.* Kind of catchy. My faux Rolex tells me the bewitching hour has arrived.

"It's almost 1:30. All the usual suspects are being rounded up. Let's head back," I suggest.

"That was a real treat. Let's try and take in a couple more vintage races. I think it would make a great article," Olivia answers.

Great minds think alike. I nod.

"I hope Hans has a plan to deal with a cast of thousands," I quip.

"You can rest assured he has everything under control."

"No doubt." My phone starts to vibrate. I look down and answer on speaker. I put up my hand to stop Olivia from getting too far ahead.

"Thomas, its Henry. I am approaching the intersection of I-95 and I-4. How do you want me to proceed? The Caddy is still behind me. They are either not good at tailing me or they want me to know they are out there."

"Assume they are good. Henry, I don't think you've been candid about things. If you want us to save your butt, you have got to be straight with us. No bull shit."

"I don't have a choice Thomas. I have run out of options."

"Close enough. Exit onto Route 92 and continue toward the track. Enter on Nascar Drive and bear left until you get to the tunnel. When you exit the tunnel . . . stop. There will be a golf cart waiting. Get in and say nothing except *Hudson Hornet.* Understand?"

"But what am I going to do about the guys in the Escalade?"

"Henry, this is not a question and answer. This is Thomas says and Henry does. Got it?"

"Loud and clear!"

"Over and out!" I end the call.

"I'll call Mike and Josh and tell them to have unmarked units waiting at either end of the tunnel. As soon as Henry is through, they'll block both ends," Detective Nederfield is in cop mode.

"Good idea. I want to call Hans now so that he can alert the backups. Tell Mike and Josh that the guys in the Escalade are very dangerous. Maybe Mike can commandeer a couple of large tow trucks to help seal the tunnel. I don't want to see a unit rammed to pieces." Olivia nods and starts dialing. I do the same. Five minutes later we resume our journey to the RV."

We arrive and are met by Maria Miello with a welcoming frosty glass of something Stanford invented. It has a coffee taste, a coconut taste and a berry taste-maybe raspberry-all pored over crushed ice with a sprig of mint. How can he do this in an RV galley kitchen?

"Merci. It is perfect," Olivia says after taking a long sip.

"They are all waiting," Maria announces.

The inside of the Ritz on wheels looks like Grand Central Station. In addition to the Bentley Seven plus one, minus Franco who is picking up Henry Fuller, the assemblage includes the McDonalds, the Miellos, Sheriff Wetherford, an RAF master sergeant and Stephen Henderson, in hand cuffs, Jung Kim, Joaquin Luis de la Herrera, Olivia and myself.

"Sheriff McCarthy is on his way," Hans announces. "He has some *amazing news.*"

"Sergeant Duffy," Sir Geoffrey begins. "You may release Mr. Henderson into our custody and are free to return to your duty. I thank you for your assistance." The hulking soldier nods, uncuffs Henderson and leaves, which only somewhat relieves the crowded condition.

"Ladies, I think we should retire to the outside kitchen. It is rather difficult to move about." Stanford gives us a Welsh smile, grabs a few things from the panty and exits.

Three go and three are about to arrive. "Please find a comfortable place to sit, if possible," Margarite suggests. "I trust you have each introduced yourselves. I think we should wait until Franco returns with Mr. Fuller. Sheriff Wetherford has been provided backup by both the team that followed Mr. Henderson and the team that followed Mr. Fuller. A SWAT team from both Volusia County and Florida Highway Patrol are being assembled. At least one armored vehicle has been dispatched from Patrick Air Force Base."

"I have made arrangements to seal the tunnel, divert track access and hopefully apprehend the drivers of the Escalade as quietly and quickly as possible. I am sending over a secure prisoner transport vehicle where we will detain these folks until we have time to interrogate them." Sheriff Mike has everything under control on his end.

I think this will go down in direct proportion to the importance the guys in the Escalade have to the overall investigation. If they are simply muscle, they will try to cut a deal. If they are further up the food chain, this might be the OK Corral in Daytona.

Suddenly the door opens and Josh McCarthy's bulk fills the doorframe. "One down."

"Sheriff McCarthy, would like a cold water or perhaps a Dr. Pepper," Margarite asks.

"Actually both. I want to savor the Dr. Pepper and quench my thirst."

"What's up old buddy?" I ask.

"One murder is solved and it has nothing to do with drugs . . . more or less. Remember when I said that I had gotten a call that Damien LeValle, Jr. had been murdered? He was assassinated. Small caliber shot in the back of the head at close range. Hands bound with tie wraps. His weapon was still holstered. Ballistics confirmed that it was the weapon used to kill Cosmo. Apparently, Damien was into Costello for some serious dough, and somehow his convoluted mind figured that if he killed Cosmo, he'd be killing his debt as well. Apparently the folks in Providence didn't see it that way."

"Josh, how do you know it was the mob and not someone else who eliminated LeValle? A thug like LeValle must have a ton of enemies."

"I am glad you asked." Josh can sometimes be a tiny bit smug. "The forensic team found a single black rose on the front seat of Damien's Caddy."

A quick look around the room confirms Josh's analysis. Several members of the group are shrugging while others are nodding. The whole purpose of a mob killing is to send a message. In this case, it was revenge pure and simple but also a signal to whomever tries to pick up the pieces of LeValle's business activities. *Better settle up.* Taking Cosmo's death out of the equation is a relief, not only to me but I think it will be a relief to Donald Montgomery as well.

Hans' cell phone beckons. He answers, but does not share the conversation. He says, "That was Franco. He has Henry Fuller and will be here in ten minutes. The Escalade tried to ram through the blockade. The tow truck was victorious. The passenger is seriously injured and may not survive. He is being transferred to a local hospital in restraints. The driver was wearing his seat belt and will be okay. He is being held in the prisoner transport vehicle."

"May I interview the driver?" Joaquin Luis de la Herrera asks. "I have been very involved with a certain drug cartel in Mexico to which I believe these men are associated."

"I'll go with him so that I can get images," Charles adds.

"I'll join them," Frederick says. "I speak fluent Spanish and most native South and Central dialects as well."

"I will have my deputies search the driver for identification, weapons and poisons. We want him to remain alive and healthy." Sheriff Mike wants this done by the books. It's his jurisdiction.

"Mike, can the wreckage be cleared out of the tunnel. Things should seem as normal as possible. The truck race begins in about thirty minutes and qualifying for the big boys begins at 4:00." I inquire.

"Already being done. The tow truck at the entrance is pulling the Caddy out and the truck at the exit is banged up, but can move on its own accord. The track is sending a street sweeper through to make sure all the debris is removed. Everything should be back to normal in fifteen minutes. Tops."

"Well done Sheriff Wetherford!" Sir Geoffrey exclaims. "Before Mr. Fuller arrives, I think we should have a chat with Mr. Henderson. Say what?"

"Sheriff, you may use my RV for your interview," Cecil offers. "Since he is a murder suspect, may I suggest Sir Geoffrey, Pierre and I accompany you? That will free up some space here for the real show." Cecil chuckles.

"Mr. Henderson, are you willing to be a good chap or shall we need to handcuff you?" Sir Geoffrey oozes with charm, but with a bite.

"I didn't do anything wrong. Sure I'll answer your questions."

The group remaining still has plenty of horsepower to interrogate Henry Fuller, who just arrives with Franco. Hans, Margarite and Jung Kim all have cards up their sleeves I suspect.

CHAPTER FIFTY-ONE

The door to the RV opens and Henry Fuller bolts through. "Thomas, I am in deep trouble." The last word is stretched out to be about four syllables as Henry looks around the room.

"That, Mr. Fuller is an understatement," Hans says as cool as a cucumber.

"Thomas, what is the meaning of this?" Henry stammers.

"Let me introduce you to our team. Well, that part of the team not otherwise engaged in interviewing Stephen Henderson and the driver of the Escalade that has been following you."

"My crew chief?" Fuller interrupts.

"Yes. He is accused of killing Harvey Silver." Henry Fuller goes from being red in the face to completely white.

"I can explain. It's a bit complicated, but I can explain."

"Before you say anything Mr. Fuller, you have the right to remain silent. Anything you say can and will be held against you in a court of law. You have the right to an attorney. If you cannot afford an attorney, one will be appointed for you." Josh returns his Miranda card to his pocket. "Do you understand?"

"Yes, I am familiar with my rights and I waive my right to have a lawyer present." Henry has resumed a matter-of-fact attitude.

"Mr. Fuller, we would like to record our interview on camera. Is that satisfactory?" Hans asks.

He nods.

"Even though your movements are being recorded we need the audio portion as well, so please answer questions by voice." Detective Nederfield wants to make sure the I's are dotted and the T's are crossed.

Franco approaches Fuller and clips a mini-microphone to his shirt collar. He puts another on Hans' shirt, Jacque Miello's tie and Jung Kim's coat. "I only have four personal microphones so everyone else has to share the hand held. Please identify yourself before speaking. We are ready to begin."

I gesture to the microphone. Hans nods. "Henry, I promised to introduce the balance of our team. You know Detective Olivia Nederfield who is standing next to Sheriff McCarthy. You've met Franco. Inspector General Jacques Miello of the Sûretè and Mr. Jung Kim of Kim Enterprises and Korean Intelligence." The latter comment causes Kim to raise his eyebrow. "And last but not least, our hosts Margarite and Hans Leiter. Henry, just so you are not taken by surprise, Inspector Herrera of Interpol, Sir Geoffrey McDonald of MI 6, Volusia County Sheriff Wetherford, team members Cecil and Charles Llewellyn, Frederick Voss and Pierre Richard, Mrs. Leiter's brother, may join us from time to time."

"I get the picture, Thomas. I am up the creek without a paddle," Henry Fuller quips.

"How far up the creek is totally up to you." Hans says. "Sorry Franco, Hans speaking. We know a lot about you Mr.

Fuller starting over twenty years ago, your self-imposed exile to Argentina, your initial relationship with Georgio Cidado, your subsequent employment by him and your drug smuggling. We need you to fill in some of the blanks, mostly who, where and when."

"They'll kill me!" Fuller cries.

"Thomas here." I am still holding the microphone. "If you don't cooperate, they definitely will kill you. Once it is made known that you met with us, the cartel will never know whether you told us anything or not. So I urge you to tell us everything. Think about it. Let me pose the following hypothetical question, if you have to go to prison where would you want to be held? Korea? Argentina? Columbia? Mexico? Or the US of A?"

"You wouldn't tell anyone that I squealed when I didn't?"

"Josh here. You can bet on it. None of us likes drugs and we really don't like drug dealers."

"What do you want?"

"This is Hans. As I said before we want the names of your contacts from whom you procure drugs, their addresses, associates, the persons to whom the drugs are delivered, the delivery routes and method of transport."

Inspector General starts to talk to his tie. "This is Miello speaking. We also want methods of payment including account numbers and access to the accounts from which you pay for the drugs and receive payment."

"Jung Kim speaking. I want to know about the specific manner in which you drop ship our tires after placing the drugs within the container. You must be working with customs officials since the shipments are under seal."

"This is Detective Nederfield. We were brought into this case because an individual was murdered and we were concerned that his death might be connected to the drug shipment that disappeared after reaching Miami on its way to Homestead. Both couriers were killed. While some of the other questions you were just asked deal with the big picture, I want a couple of answers now."

"May I have some water?"

"Oui." Margarite hands a bottle to Henry who almost drops it.

"I am associated with the Columbian drug cartel, Modero, which is trying to enter the Mexican market. The Mexican cartels are smaller and there is a lot of in-fighting, but they have united in their hatred of Modero. Long and short, the two couriers were murdered because they were delivering cocaine from Modero to me. I can transport large amounts by hiding the smack in Kim tires that I ship all over the West Coast. But my cost of doing business is very high and I am a middleman and don't reap the real profits on the retail side. I was intending to hide the coke in tires which we take back and forth to races. The murders were a warning to me. I assumed that Modero would protect my backside, but I found out through the grapevine that I was expendable in part because I am a Gringo and in part because Kim is re-structuring its distribution system and Southern California was being reassigned to a new distributor. So basically I was flying solo with some very bad people pissed off at me." Fuller's pseudo sophisticated façade is rapidly peeling away.

"What about the screw in the tire?" Olivia asks.

"I'm not sure. I figured that it was another warning, but from whom? I went to confront Harvey Silver, our tire guy. He got real defensive and came after me with a heavy tire iron. I was able to grab one end and we struggled. It was tug of war. Harvey was pulling so hard that I had to let go, the bar swung back and hit him in the forehead. He dropped like a rock. I panicked. I picked up the bar. I realized that Harvey was not moving. I grabbed a rag and wiped off the bar where I had been holding it and put it dropped it next to the tire machine and took off. I don't understand what Steve Henderson has to do with it. The whole thing was an accident."

"Quite so," Sir Geoffrey says entering the RV followed by Sheriff Mike and Cecil. "By the way Cecil, these micro receivers have wonderful acoustics."

I notice that all three have tiny little ears buds.

"May I assume that you heard everything you needed to hear?" Hans says.

"My powers of observation tell me that Mr. Henderson is not amongst you."

"He's actually on his way over to the Team Fuller garage. The damage to Juan Carlos' car is very superficial and the pit crew is getting it ready for qualifying tomorrow, although they are short a driver." Cecil is always well informed.

"First things first," Josh says. "What about the dead guy, Harvey what's his name?"

"Coroner's report basically backs up what Mr. Fuller said about the tire iron injury, but that's not what killed him. Mr. Silver had congenital heart failure. Apparently he had several episodes recently, but did not seek medical advice. When he basically hit himself in the head with the pipe, he experienced a massive heart attack. He was dead before he hit the ground."

"Henry, it seems that you actually told the truth." I can be mean at times, but Fuller's drug connection and the consequences to everyone and everything is unforgiveable.

"Why did Stephen Henderson panic?" Olivia asks.

"Apparently he and the now widow Silver were an item. He was afraid that it would look like he killed Harvey because he was having an affair with his wife," Sheriff Wetherford recites.

"The old motive and opportunity scenario," I suggest.

"So both murders in our respective jurisdiction have been solved. Right, Mike?"

"Messieurs, while you have done your jobs admirably, and the cause of two deaths has been resolved, let me remind you that we still have a lot of ground to cover with Mr. Fuller and the gentlemen who were following him. I feel the scope of your jurisdiction expanding, including that of Detective Nederfield and Deputy Ballard. Many assets may be required in short order and I am simply too tired to explain the situation to someone else. Understood?"

Mike and Josh are standing with their mouths open. I get it. "Kind of like once on the team, always on the team?"

"Well said, Thomas. I think we should wait a few minutes until Frederick, Pierre, Charles and Mr. de la Herrera return, which should be very soon." Margarite has spoken.

"I hear my services being summonsed," Stanford says opening the door, followed by Anne and Maria, each with a tray of cookies and drinks, including Dr. Pepper.

"Did you hear anyone call for Stanford?" I whisper to Olivia.

She shakes her head and whisper back, "Don't ask."

CHAPTER FIFTY-TWO

Within a matter of about five minutes we are joined by the balance of the team.

"Buona sera! Have you had a very interesting experience?"

"Charles, here is a Perrier. You must be parched." Stanford hands him a bottle. "Please gentlemen, help yourself."

De la Herrera looks quite uncomfortable. Margarite as usual picks up the vibes. "Everyone here is very familiar with the workings of law enforcement at every possible level. You can be candid and forthright with everyone here, except Mr. Fuller, but we have an understanding, don't we monsieur?" Margarite stares in Henry's direction. He looks like he is going to pass out.

"I understand . . . perfectly."

"Très bon."

"Charles, I am running your photos through the system." Hans inserts. "Mr. de la Herrera, will give us a summary?"

"Yes, Sir. When we arrived the passenger was being removed from the SUV. He was rather badly hurt. He started speaking to the other man in a language I did not understand. Dr. Voss was familiar with the dialect and the three spoke for several minutes. The EMTs secured his release from the vehicle and he was taken to a hospital. The other man exited the vehicle without incident. He was searched. We found no weapon. Identification was removed from his person and placed in an evidence bag. Dr. Voss and the man continued to speak for another minute or so and then switched to speaking in Spanish which we all understood. I am frankly amazed at the multiple skills you possess."

Olivia gives me a little pinch in the butt. Duh.

"May I?" Frederick asks. "I was able to communicate with the men in their native tongue which gave me a certain level of credibility. They are brothers from Oaxaca, Mexico and sometimes are asked to do errands for a number of cartels, mostly surveillance. The driver, Benito, has been very forthright in exchange for my assurance that his brother would receive the best medical treatment. They were hired to follow Mr. Fuller and report his movements. They were told not to intercept him, but simply text his location every hour. He was worried because it had been an hour since he last checked in. I told him to text our location at the race track, except we used the coordinates for the small group of green garages at the far end of the track property. Sheriff Wetherford, I hope you don't mind but I asked your SWAT team and a few deputies to take up strategic positions on the site. Sir Geoffrey, I requested a few of your chaps to join them. Seemed to make them very happy. Benito also said that he believed that he and his brother had been followed. He is concerned about conflict regarding Mr. Fuller. I did not dissuade him. He is being transported to the hospital under guard and then will be held for further questioning."

"How are we going to bait the trap and who do you expect to snare?" I ask.

"Excellent question Thomas. Any ideas?" Hans replies.

"May I?" Jung Kim asks. "We have many moving parts in this investigation. I am pleased that you have removed two deaths from the equation although neither seems related to the larger issues."

"Actually, at one time you were a suspect in the murder of Cosmo Costello, who was more than tangentially connected to the drug world." Detective Nederfield's beautiful blues eyes turn icy cold.

"Me? That's ridiculous. I met the man only once and tried to convince him to use Kim tires on his nephew's car. He wanted to make sure the tires were safe and rule compliant. I agreed and delivered all the material as you know." Kim is very matter of fact. "I did not know he had died until about sixty seconds ago. I thought I was to meet him this morning. His nephew agreed to race on the Kim tires and won the race. Virtually no one knows of my relationship with our government, so when Mr. Ballard introduces me as a member of the intelligence community I realized that my cover was no longer a secret and then I looked around this room and understood why."

"May I ask a question?" Franco raises his hand like a fourth grader wanting to get e bathroom pass.

"Yes, of course," Jung Kim responds.

"I have been very bothered by Kim Tires being a part of Kim Enterprises. It seems too far from your central business. Sì?"

"Very simple. A family friend came to my brother with a company to sell, a facility that sold specialized tires for various applications. He had developed a unique product and made great use of technology in manufacturing. He needed a lot of capital to go to the next level, which was making and selling performance tires. My brother made him an offer he couldn't refuse. Our friend is still CEO of the company and has a very nice compensation package. I have been associated with various groups within our government since I graduated business school. Our family is very much connected and by using the tire company as a front, I could get access to information primarily about the distribution of drugs. We spread a lot of misinformation about the cloaking effect of tires to see if a major cocaine cartel would bite. They did and we are closing the net upon some very bad and dangerous people. We certainly think that Mr. Fuller would be well served to help. I was not aware of the scope of this investigation until I got here and met you."

"Excuse me for asking, but you really seem to like the tire side of your business." I observe.

"I do. I think it is cool to build something outside the box. Whether it be in computer sciences or the design and manufacturing of a tire."

"I think the landscape is fairly well defined, but now we have to spring one trap, which I suspect will yield the killers of the courier. Then with Mr. Fuller's help, spin a very large web to entangle a lot of spiders from a lot of different places." Sir Geoffrey is very succinct.

"But first we must attend to some very immediate issues. What bait can we offer to several cold blooded murders?" I look around the room. Everyone is looking at Henry Fuller. A Judas goat.

The pause in conversation lasts less than five seconds but it seems like five minutes and is broken by a loud knocking on the door of Hotel Bentley.

"Please enter," Our hostess says.

"Pardon. I wanted to report that the men I was asked to apprehend have been secured without bloodshed." Master Sergeant Duffy salutes in that unique British way.

"Please elaborate Sergeant," Sir Geoffrey asks.

"Dr. Voss asked my men and some chaps from the Sheriff's office to set up a surveillance perimeter around the garages at the far end of the track. He told me to expect two maybe three men to arrive and try to gain access. They were to be taken alive for interrogation. The manner of doing so was left to my discretion. When we got to the site most everyone was positioned about. One of your SWAT fellows was very cleaver with electricity and wired all the lights into a remote control except one at the far end, where I stood, mostly in shadow, back to the door. About fifteen minutes later the door opened and two men wearing all black entered and slowly approached me. Suddenly the garage was lighted like a Christmas tree. The two blokes in black pulled out flick knives. Each of the men inside the building aimed their weapon. I slowly turned around. My father once told me; never bring a knife to a gun fight. I guess no one told those two. My orders were to bring them back alive and it was looking a bit dicey when two of my men, Gurkhas who we were training with us, stepped forward and drew their knives. The two with the flickers were not stupid. Anyone who uses a knife knows about Gurkhas. Well they dropped their knives and placed their hands on their heads, were tie wrapped and are waiting at the garage."

"Splendid work. Splendid," Sir Geoffrey says. Everyone is delighted, in part, since no one was killed. Paperwork and all that.

"I suggest Mr. de la Herrera and I stroll down to the garages with the sergeant," Frederick suggests.

"May I join?" Sheriff Wetherford asks.

Hans nods.

I am about to ask whether the DEA should be involved in the interrogation, but I conclude that others know more than I do about multi jurisdictional investigations and I elect to keep my mouth shut.

"Hopefully the gentlemen in the garage are the same as those who killed the couriers and that they have more information to offer than the two in the Escalade," Cecil reflects.

"I expect they will tell us everything they know. The quantity and quality of their information will have to be scrutinized," Jacque Miello suggests.

"Henry, my friend," I try not to gag. "There are many people here and I suspect others, who will want to talk with you. Hans, I think that Mr. Fuller needs to be transferred to a place more conducive to a rather lengthy interrogation."

"Thomas, it has already been attended to. A safe house has been set up. Mr. Fuller, you will be secure but you are expected to be forthright. If we feel that you are not, you will be transferred to a supermax prison and await either processing in the United States or extradition to any one of a number of countries. The only people who will know your location will be those who absolutely need to know. Most of the investigative team will be without knowledge of your location. Your protection will be provided by very skilled people. Do you understand?"

"Yes."

"Monsieur Fuller, we have many times interviewed people who have unique insight into our investigations. We are very good at what we do. Please do not try to tell us what you think we want to hear. If you tell us everything and provide access to documents, we will advocate on your behalf. We cannot guarantee that you will not go to prison, but we can guarantee that we will treat you fairly, provided that you do not try to, what is the word, hoodwink us. It will not work."

"I understand. I take full responsibility for what I have done and will cooperate fully. Thank you all for your civility. I have lost my way. Maybe I never was on the right path."

Yet another knock on the door interrupts Henry Fuller's presentation.

"Entrer!" Pierre says.

"I hope I am not disturbing anything. Mr. Fuller, we did exactly what Mr. Llewellyn told us to do. We found Mr. Montgomery and made the adjustments to the Camaro so that he could drive the car. He is very excited. The Chief Steward checked number 31 and agrees that the damage is minimal so we won't be penalized and have to start at the rear. We can qualify tomorrow morning since the 4 o'clock qualifying has been cancelled."

"Cancelled?" I ask.

"There is lightning forecasted for the next two hours and the truck race starts at 6:00."

Everyone looks at Cecil. He shrugs.

"Thomas, will you look after the team? It's fully funded for the rest of the season. Maybe you can do some testing for Kim tires. I know that you have always wanted to be a NASCAR team owner." Henry Fuller has a wicked smile on his face.

"You know Henry; I might take you up on your offer. Young Montgomery might be exactly what the team needs; a real hands on owner/driver. But Olivia and I get to sit in the crew chief's box."

Also by D.G. Stern

The Adventures of Upton Charles—Dog Detective

Disappearing Diamonds
Something Fishy
Winter Wonderland
Lost Loot
Ship Shape
Tip Top
Picture Perfect
Time Tale

And coming soon
Missing Map

Also

The Loneliest Tree
25 Days of a Tropical Christmas
Francis the Firehouse Mouse
Sophie the Skunk
Hot Tea . . . Cold Case
There's Always Tomorrow
Stabbing Along the Straightaway
Chaos at the Concours

And coming soon
Look into the Mirror
Critical Corner
Iced Tea . . . Warm Corpse

Visit us on the web at:
www.neptunepress.org

www.ingramcontent.com/pod-product-compliance
Lightning Source LLC
Chambersburg PA
CBHW022154170626
46807CB00005B/2209

* 9 7 8 1 7 3 2 4 5 5 1 2 2 *